Wondering, the Way is Made

A South American Odyssey

by

Luke F. D. Marsden

First Edition

Published by Speaking Eye Press

Copyright © 2015 Luke F. D. Marsden

All rights reserved.

ISBN 978-0-9933229-0-7

For wanderers and wonderers

ACKNOWLEDGEMENTS

I am grateful to John Pomphrey, David O'Flaherty, David Allan and Victoria Brown, without whom this book would not exist in its present form.

PREFACE

I first got the idea for Wondering, the Way is Made when I was in Kerala, India in the summer of 2011. There was a deadly heatwave at that time in the US. It was a summer of riots in the UK. From a distance I watched and, with a small step of the imagination, envisioned what it would be like if things degenerated to the point where it was no longer worth returning home.

I eventually came to write the book some years later, whilst in South America. Many of the situations, background events and anecdotes in it are closely based on reality, even though some of them may seem far-fetched. This is also the case for the locations - all of them are places that I visited along my way. The far-flung and far-fetched can be far nearer than we realise.

Luke F. D. Marsden

I

"What I am saying is that we must get them their battery by tomorrow. This is an emergency situation! Their car *must be fixed* by tomorrow morning, before it is too late."

The kind-faced old man, tall, smartly dressed, with white hair and a white beard, addressed the group of two dozen or so villagers, most sitting, some standing, in the shade beneath a wide acacia tree.

"But, Robinson, why can't they just wait three or four days until a new battery arrives?"

~~~~~

We were lucky that the gate to the Murchison Falls National Park had been closed when we had arrived there just after dusk the previous evening. Also that the boy on the gate with the AK47 had been so charmingly naïve that he failed even to notice our unsubtle attempts at bribery to persuade him to let us in. Breaking down in the deep jungle at night would have put us in a serious predicament.

As it was, we drove a few minutes back in the direction of the nearest town until we saw the sign for a "Women's Run" guesthouse. We drove in and stopped the car on the muddy driveway. As we got out of the car, a lady, who looked to be in her fifties, came outside and greeted us in the usual Ugandan style. Hello, how are you? I'm well, thanks, how are you? I'm well, thanks.

She told us her name was Edna and gave us a little of the history of the place. It had been established by the government a couple of years earlier as a non-profit venture run only by women. Edna had been managing it on her own ever since. By day it doubled as a school. Would we like to stay? Yes, just for one night.

She ushered us into a reception room and disappeared for a few minutes before returning with mugs of herbal tea. We talked about the journey from Kampala. Was it long? Longer than it should have been after we got lost attempting to follow directions to the only garage in Kampala that sold ice, and ended up asking bemused villagers where the nearest freezer was. This story delighted Edna, who found it so funny she asked us to write it down in a book that she used to record visitors' comments, good wishes and anecdotes. It was as we were writing that we had heard the front door open and a voice boom "HELLO!" The old man had walked in smiling with a "Hello, Mrs. Edna!" before looking at us and back at her.

"Oh," Edna said with a start. "This is Robinson. He's our maintenance man."

"And security guard!" added Robinson tapping the empty gun holster at his waist. He either hadn't noticed the missing weapon or didn't consider it of any importance.

He sat down in an armchair and started to tell us, without any reduction in the volume of his voice, about himself. He had worked for a long time as a guide in the Ugandan National Park Authority before retiring a few years earlier. As a guide, he had got to know many *mzungus*, their customs and how to keep them happy. In addition to being Edna's handyman and security guard he was her advisor in the curious ways of foreigners.

He stopped talking and frowned at our mugs then stood up and left the room. Edna smiled at us nervously. Robinson returned with a box of red wine and some plastic cups. He undoubtedly was familiar with *mzungus* and their ways. With the exception of Edna, we all served ourselves some wine and toasted. Robinson told us about what we could expect to see at Murchison Falls and advised us to set off half an hour before dawn because early morning was the only time the animals came out of hiding.

We told him of how we had planned to be in the park already, and how it was that we had come to be here. When he heard about the search for ice he didn't laugh like Edna had done. He just nodded understandingly. Normal *mzungu* behaviour, no doubt.

Then it started to rain heavily.

"I see you parked the car up in front of the house. If it rains too much, it will get stuck. You should move it to the road."

I took the keys and walked out across the heavy red mud to the car. When I turned them in the ignition, nothing happened. I cursed silently and tried again, and again. There was nothing to be done, the battery was completely dead. I went back with the news.

~~~~~

"But, Robinson, why can't they just wait three or four

days until a new battery arrives?" petitioned Edna, who sat at the front of the group and wore a blue headscarf. A meeting of the guesthouse community had been called in the morning to resolve our issue with the battery. It had been impossible to get anything done the previous night, before first light, so we would leave for the falls first thing the next day. In the meantime, Robinson had promised he would take it upon himself to get our car running again.

He looked as though he had been expecting Edna's question, and before answering he drew himself up to his full height with the air of a university professor lecturing on his specialist field. The audience was attentive as he spoke, projecting his voice such that we could hear his words clearly even from where we were sitting on the veranda of the guesthouse.

"Mrs. Edna, there is something you must understand about *mzungus*, which is that they have something known as a *programme*." He paused to allow this to register with his listeners. "Do you know what a *programme* is?"

"No," replied Edna, who clearly did know, but wanted Robinson to begin his explanation from first principles.

"Well, you see, Mrs. Edna, let me explain it like this. Instead of doing one thing until it is finished, and then thinking 'What will I do next?' and moving on to the next thing, a *mzungu* will know *exactly what he is going to do, and when he is going to do it, for the whole week.* Maybe two weeks! This is a programme."

He drew up his chin and peered expectantly along the length of his nose, awaiting a reaction from his crowd to this great revelation.

"Oh," said Edna. Her forehead creased as she

processed the idea of westerners planning in advance exactly what they were going to do with every moment of their lives. Others in the crowd wore frowns too. Maybe this would turn out to be the key to explaining why they were all so strange. She gave up. "Why do they do that?" she asked.

"Because…" began Robinson, looking over at us and winking, "because with a programme they can do many more things in the same amount of time! That's the reason why *mzungu* countries make so much money!"

Edna nodded, still frowning. "So a programme is something that we should have too?" There was animated discussion in corners of the group, which had grown in numbers since a few passers-by had paused to hear Robinson speak.

"Please, please!" asked Robinson, motioning for quiet. Stillness descended once more, only the scratching of the cicadas breaking the silence. "You ask why we don't have a programme, well let me tell you. Programmes are very useful, as I have just explained, but they are not for everyone. Sometimes they can go *bad.*"

"Really?" Edna was listening intently to every word.

"Yes. You see, *mzungus* make these programmes because in their countries they know that everything will work correctly. And when they come to Uganda they still make their programmes but they forget that things don't work here like they do when they are at home. And then when something goes wrong, like there's no petrol, or the road has been flooded, or the battery doesn't work, they can't do all the things in their programme. Sometimes, even when they are at home, the programme doesn't work. At these times, when the programme goes bad, it makes them very unhappy. *Very unhappy.* Sometimes angry!"

Edna took a sharp breath and looked at us, wide eyed. Then she relaxed. We didn't seem like the type to get angry. Her face turned to concern as she realised that, in that case, we must be the kind who got sad. "Oh dear!" She turned back to Robinson, who was not finished.

"So now you see, Mrs. Edna, it is very important that we fix these *mzungus'* car by tomorrow morning, before it is too late."

There it was. *Quod erat demonstrandum.* I looked around at my friends at this moment. We had been sipping on some cold beers that had been magicked to us, with the assistance of Robinson no doubt. Opposite me, across the table, Joe, an imposing graduate of philosophy and the Robinson figure of our group, looked awestruck, as though he had just witnessed something extremely profound. At the far corner, Neil, his hard-working, hard-playing older brother, was organising the purchase of some more beers and a box of ice with the lad who had brought us the previous round, and had missed most of what had gone on. To my right, Mark, a burly Canadian who was unable to take anything seriously, was already making a joke of it.

"Ey, *mzungu!*" He directed himself at Neil, "My beer's empty and the next one's not here. This is interfering with my *programme*, man!"

Neil looked at him quizzically, his shock of messy blond hair comically enhancing the effect, and extended his quarter-full beer. "Cool it, Redface, they're coming. In the meantime try holding this one to your forehead so your face doesn't explode."

Mark was known as Redface, or most often just Red, for his red hair, red beard and red complexion. The Ugandan heat and sunshine had made him twice as red as usual. Before Neil could react, he had snatched the oversize bottle of beer from his hand and drained it, emitting a self-satisfied sigh and beer-burp as he leaned back in his chair. Neil kicked his chair leg from under the table, knocking him over backwards, then jumped on top of him. A small scuffle ensued on the ground.

Joe leaned over and fixed my eye. "It's so *simple*, but *genius*. Why hadn't I seen it?"

Without waiting for my reply, he raised his great frame from the chair and went to talk with Robinson, walking over to the acacia tree and catching his shoulder with a strong paw as people began to disperse.

Myself, looking back, I can see that Robinson's words resonated with something deep within me. I absorbed the scene around us, as though knowing I would come to recount it some day: my friends wrestling on the ground, the still heat and the shade of the trees, Joe and Robinson laughing together at some shared words, the pleasantly sour bite of the beer on my tongue, a nice smile from the tall daughter of Mrs. Edna as she passed. While I may not have been aware of it at that moment, it was then that I decided to step out of the *programme*.

~~~~~

Following the meeting, Robinson formulated a plan of action. His friend from the town, who owned a bike, would come from there in the afternoon, and we would give him our dead battery and fifty dollars. He would then take it back to town and either get it fixed or buy another used one. Then, he would come back with the battery and the remaining money early enough the next morning to allow us to get on our way on time, keeping three dollars for his troubles. It was a good plan, we all agreed. Beaming, Robinson went to retrieve the box of wine again.

"Now let's all have a drink to celebrate!" which we did.

The next morning we overslept. So did Robinson and his friend with the bike. We awoke in the guesthouse to the sound of schoolchildren singing, which is something that one cannot plan for. The park would still be there, and the falls would still be falling, tomorrow.

II

"Joss?" the voice of Tina broke my slumber. I opened my eyes and saw her curiously inspecting my face close up, her tousled afro blocking out the sun. "Let's do something this afternoon."

I stretched, sleepy from my early siesta, "Yep, good idea. What are you thinking?"

"Bikes! We can get them while the tide's out."

"Cool, we'll go in five."

I gradually came to, the mist in my head lifting with the sun's rays streaming in rainbows through my eyelashes. While dozing, my mind had played back the discussion over my resignation from my job. They hadn't liked it. I had spoken with the programme manager, Miles Warren M.B.A, as the nameplate on his desk announced. He had kept asking me to take time to reconsider. His face stuck in my mind. It was expressive, elastic and grotesque, like a gargoyle. As the face and jowls moved, the eyes remained fixed, as though controlled by gyroscopes. They were the eyes of a fish in an ice tray, betraying nothing, unblinkingly awaiting input, swallowing everything that entered. I had politely explained, using the kind of empty platitudes that organisations of that type like to use themselves when lying to their workers, that my mind was made up. I expressed that I had enjoyed my time there, but that now it was time for me to move on, and requested again that he accept my letter. Once more, I received solicitations to reconvene when I had taken time to think over everything we had discussed – possible promotion, offers of more pay and so forth. We were at an impasse. The face of Miles Warren M.B.A. wore a satisfied expression, like a problem had been solved. It was an effort to stop myself from laughing.

I knew something of the history of Miles Warren M.B.A. He was a typical cross-product of management self-help literature, of the kind that is found in abundance at airports, and the primitive reward system that was operated by the company. A mediocre and unimposing engineer who had struggled in his early career with complex tasks, he had gravitated towards project management, where the grossly simplified world of Gantt charts and Red-Amber-Green weekly status reports had appealed to him. Finally having found something he understood, he had grown in confidence and risen through the ranks of middle management. Mysteriously, this rise through the hierarchy had been matched by an accompanying physical transformation. Like a lower primate who finds himself as a dominant male in a social group and awakens one morning to discover that a bright blue vulva has appeared on his chest, Miles Warren M.B.A. had, with his most recent promotion, almost overnight developed a thick neck, heavier build and an affected air of gravitas that partnered the sense of self-importance he now carried. No doubt, he really did believe he was doing something important. The best liars are those that believe their own lies. Even there, in that office, expecting to be lied to, I had to concentrate to see through this deluded individual's performance and the eleventh-hour promises that would be forgotten as quickly as he made them.

"OK, no need to meet again. I've considered everything we've talked about and I've reached a decision," I announced. There was only one way to go.

"Go on."

I took time to savour the moment and his expectation. "I'll go and give the letter to Human Resources myself and save you the walk so you're not detained from playing with your Gantt charts and bollocksing things up, and having meetings with your great chums and laughing at your boss' jokes and deluding yourself that you're worth something and whatever the hell else it is that you do in here. In the meantime the rest of the engineers and I can go on sorting out the filthy mess you've made of the programme."

This was met with a stern face. I imagined steam coming out of the ears. There was even, perhaps, a faint glimmer of anger in the fish eyes. Bull's eye. Not only had I burned my bridges, but nuked them.

"Don't come back tomorrow," I heard the retort as I left the door.

~~~~~

"Joss?!" Tina playfully nudged my arm and made me start. "All is good on planet Josster?" she asked. I was prone to drift off into daydreams.

"Sorry babe. Yes, I'm sound."

"Grand. Then let's go!"

We took the elongated beach cruiser bikes we had hired along the firm sand to the old, white, Portuguese fortress a couple of miles up the coast. We sat on the rocks outside the thick walls and I pulled the binoculars from my backpack. It was a good place to see dolphins. They made their way through the channel dividing the Ilha do Mel, where we were, from the Ilha Peças, to the north.

"First one to see a dolphin," I challenged.

Tina screwed up her face. "You only have the advantage of the binoculars, but it's cool, we're still on."

"You can have them if you want, they normally come through quite close, between us and that rock with the light on it."

"Whatevs." Her stubbornness would not allow her to take them.

Tina had left her job, too, before we had come away. She had worked in the law, the wrong profession, her independent spirit clashing with the world of unachievable billing targets that demanded total self-sacrifice and eroded the soul. She had embraced my suggestion that we leave the *programme* behind us, delightfully, and we had got engaged. Having Afro-Brazilian roots from a father who had died before she could know him, she had long held an ambition to go to Brazil and she set about making it happen. And here we were, now, on a beach, on a magical island in the South Atlantic Ocean.

"Dolphins! Look, there are five of them at least!"

Daydreaming again, I had not been paying proper attention to watching for dolphins, instead scanning the rows of container ships offshore, stretching back to the eastern horizon. We had seen them at night. With their bridges lit up, in the dark, they resembled a floating city. At those times, further to the north, shone the bright lights of the fishing vessels. In India, I remembered, the fishermen's nets had often been torn to pieces by shoals of puffer fish. Attracted to the nets by the struggling catch, they themselves would become entangled and cut themselves free with their hard teeth.

The dolphins swam unhurriedly past us, disappearing when a fisherman in a loud motor boat sped past them, heading in the opposite direction. Tina was looking at me triumphantly. I could see she was resisting the urge to do her standard victory dance, most likely because she had lost our game of chess earlier that day. "And… what do I win? You were nowhere even close," she asked.

"A hug?" I volunteered.

"What?!" she feigned disappointment, "We're going to have to finalise the small print before we do any more of these."

"I've said before – don't go all legal on me. You're not at work now."

We laughed and ate the sandwiches we had prepared from the breakfast spread at the *pousada*, where we were staying. I inspected my feet. A few weeks into our journey, the great physical and mental benefits of not working were already becoming apparent. No longer bound for most of the day in layers of cotton and leather, they had angrily flared red at first, as their athlete's foot resisted the sand and salt water that now touched them. They were returning to natural tones as it faded and died. Away from the inveigling glow of computer screens and the slow torture of white noise from air-conditioning units and open-plan offices, my eyesight had become sharper, my thoughts clearer and my dreams more vivid. I walked taller and straighter. I was tuning into the myriad channels of nature and our surroundings. I felt a stronger connection to Tina. She, too, looked better than ever. Her eyes were clearer and brighter, and she had turned a radiant hazelnut-brown.

I looked out towards an empty part of the ocean. We had come to the hundreds of miles of beaches of southern Brazil, arriving via Buenos Aires and overland from there through Uruguay, for R&R, nothing more, resisting the urge to make a *programme* for ourselves. When rested, we would move on. A sailboat appeared as a tiny white point in my field of view. I observed its effortless progress for a while with the binoculars, wondering where it was going.

We cycled further around the empty northern coast of the island for a couple of hours until we came to a pack of black vultures around a turtle on the sand. There was a strict hierarchy amongst them. Only one would peck the flesh at a time. The deference that the others displayed while this was happening seemed strange to me. We watched and waited for an argument but there was none. They were wary of us. There was one that looked like Miles Warren M.B.A, turkey-like, not eating, just looking at me. I found it disconcerting and chased it several hundred yards down the beach.

"What was that about?" asked Tina, when I came back.

"That one was a bastard," I replied, panting. "He wanted to eat me." I ignored Tina's bemused expression.

Conscious of the rising tide, we turned around and rode back around the coast, past the white fortress and, beyond that, past toppled trees and wooden houses with makeshift sea defences of sandbags and plastic sheets, everything slowly falling into the ocean.

III

That evening, we sat on the bay side of the island sharing a big bottle of beer while watching the sun set. It illuminated the bay pink from behind the forested mountains of the Serra do Mar, before darkness fell and the lights of the shipyard on the mainland and the red and green flashes of the shipping lane came to life.

We ordered squid and pasta from one of the places in the village, thanking the healthy old lady who ran it as she brought the food to us. *Obrigado.*

"*¿Donde são voçes?*" she asked, looking at Tina. I spoke Spanish but my Portuguese was broken, comprising Spanish peppered with Portuguese words and phrases. Tina had been learning for just a few weeks. I replied as best as I could on her behalf.

"From England, both of us."

She turned to me, surprised, "*¡Opa!* She looks like a *Brasileira!*"

"Yes, she's *media Brasileira*, but this is the first time she's in Brazil."

"She speaks Portuguese?"

"*Muito Poco.*"

She looked at Tina again with an expression like she had just bitten on a sour plum, but then relaxed back into her natural, cheerful face. Tina was scowling at me, she didn't like it when I told the locals of her Brazilian connections. The proprietress defused the situation.

"*¡Está muita bonita!*"

Tina understood this compliment and gave her a beaming smile. Before she could say anything more the woman exclaimed loudly, "*¡Olhe!* Look! England!"

She was pointing at an old television set mounted in a corner of the open wooden structure, up by the ceiling. I looked at it over my shoulder. The pictures showed buildings on fire, traffic jams, crowds of masked and hooded people rioting and the plods carrying guns and tazers. I looked over at Tina, who looked shocked. "*Again*," she said.

"Looks like normal!" I joked to the old lady, who cackled and teetered off. The television had switched to showing our politicians talking BS with affected gravitas, this much was evident even without the volume turned up. Never trust anyone who projects gravitas. I looked back at Tina. "We'll have to find out what's going on."

"Why did you tell her I was half Brazilian?" she shot back.

"Because it's difficult to explain why you look Brazilian without mentioning that. And I wanted to see, for another time, that puckered-up expression of distaste they do when they find out you don't speak Portuguese. They think you're one of theirs. You need to get on it."

I mimicked the sour plum look and fixed her with it. She remained impassive.

~~~~~

We strolled along to the internet shack after eating. It was nothing more than a big shed with a few machines and a teenager on a desk by the door. There was a queue.

"Doesn't seem so bright now not bringing your mobile, does it, brains? You could have just used the wifi at the pousada."

Tina had recovered some of her sense of humour, evidently. I had consciously gone off the grid before making the trip out here, including discarding my cellphone.

"It's no biggie, I'll just wait. Head back if you like."

"Alright, I'm going to make some calls just to check that everyone's alright, so you can take your time," she said, blowing a kiss as she meandered off, shoulders drawn back and hips swaying under her light cotton dress.

I got myself a large and bitter *limão* juice from a place opposite and sipped on it as I waited my turn. I felt reluctant to reconnect with the real world but, in spite of myself, my curiosity had been piqued by the images from earlier. No, *this* was the real world, I corrected myself.

The news from the other world was sadly familiar. It was July, summer in the Northern Hemisphere, more disorder in the UK, the usual wildfires in North America, the Mediterranean, Scandinavia and Russia. Some years there was a respite, most years they got worse. This time there were tracts of Siberia and Canada the size of England on fire and only the coming of Winter would put them out. There was already barely any ice left in the Arctic Ocean. In Britain, there was a heat wave and a haze of smog. People rioted and stockpiled. In other countries, it was the same. The economic crisis caused by high food and oil prices was getting worse, the ostensible cause of the unrest. To my mind, it was more a manifestation of a subconscious, visceral malaise. It came from a dying environment and a forgotten generation of highly educated, under-employed and disillusioned youth, burdened with debts to the banks and debts to the planet that it would never pay off.

I read for a long time. I felt a mild sense of personal aggrievement, like I had somehow been wronged, but I was glad to have the good fortune not to be at home. I turned to the preppers' forums for amusement. This collection of characters on the periphery, living in a state of constant readiness for a breakdown of law and order, must be about the only set of people with anything to be positive about, went my thinking. Every year, there were those who thought that "this was it". Sometime soon, I was sure they would be right.

"BRING IT ON!!!!!!!!!" blared one overweight, shaven-headed individual pictured in paintball fatigues. This instantly improved my mood and I could not repress a smirk. Here was a man for whom an apocalypse was clearly preferable to his ordinary, quotidian existence. There were more contributions along similar lines, and then the "this is it" contingent.

A type with a serious face from Taunton: "Bugging out. Good luck everyone."

A lady from Norfolk: "Close your eyes and count to

ten, people… ;)"

I imagined hundreds of people descending on every pot-hole in the Brecon Beacons, being surprised to see each other there, and then turning around surreptitiously and returning home in embarrassment. Then, another post caught my eye. This one was thoughtful and considered, from someone anonymous in Cumbria. It stayed with me:

"This is the hardest decision I've ever made, but I'm pressing the button and taking the family. When do you do it? That's the question. Well, three homes on the road have been robbed by lads with axes and shotguns already and there's nowt being done about it. It's out of control. There's no second chance if you leave it too late, but you can come back if you jump the gun. Thanks to all for your good advice and tips over the years, it's been well worth being considered a nut-job by my wife and kids all this time. lol."

IV

When I was six years old, both my parents died swimming off a deserted beach in Cornwall. I had been playing in some rock pools nearby when they were carried away. When I realised they were not coming back, I hid among the rocks until I was found by the coast guard the next day, wrapped in my father's shirt and jumper.

From that time on, I was raised by my grandmother, a small, submissive woman, who kept an immaculate but sad house and who rarely smiled. The best of her that I can say, looking back, is that she was conscientious and well-intentioned. I held her in great regard and did as she said, treating every word she uttered as the unquestionable truth. I studied hard at school, played sport, kept my room clean and later took evening and summer jobs that she arranged for me. "Your mother wouldn't approve," is what she would tell me if I wanted to do something that wasn't to her liking. Being a child and barely remembering my mother, I was in no position to disagree. She took away my books and replaced them with ones that she had chosen herself. She insisted on selecting all of my shoes and clothes for me. I was reprimanded for such things as leaving the shower adjusted to the wrong height and eating garlic. She hardly ever mentioned my father.

I put being bullied at school down to the other children not having the benefit of a proper upbringing such as mine. I felt I had a good life, but I was not able to be happy. Each time I felt laughter rising in me, it would be suffocated before surfacing by a great weight in my chest. On the rare occasions it broke through, it would be cut short. I had no success with girls, and my grandmother never broached the subject. I spoke little but read and observed much, unconsciously compensating, I suppose, for the lack of those millions of things, large and small, that would normally be learned from one's mother or father: the best way to run, the names of different birds and insects, how people behave, the rules of chess, how to draw, how to shave. This way I learned, little by little, and far behind my contemporaries, the way the world worked. With age I became conscious of being an observer, worked at it, and became better at it. Like an oyster, I filtered millions of tiny morsels of information from the nutrient-rich waters of my environment. These fed me, helped me grow, and hardened over time into the pearls of learning. The waters took on a new and ever-increasing clarity. The lessons that we teach and discover ourselves take root far deeper than those we are taught by others.

By the time my grandmother died, when I was at university, I knew that much of what she had told me was wrong and that most of her advice had been bad. I also knew by then that it can sometimes be good to receive bad advice. I lamented a childhood of thousands of missed opportunities, of ill-informed and misdirected actions, lived without self-confidence, and still felt the pain of the loss of my parents. I was grateful at the same time to have emerged the other side strong and with no-one to answer to. I resolved to be happy and I became so. I thirsted for the future and for the present, to make up for lost time. If you understood the world and its arcane rules, life became a game – I could do what I wanted.

I first used my knowledge to make my own life easier. I invested the inheritance from my grandmother, and using a rudimentary understanding of human nature to look for signs of herd mentality, irrational exuberance or despair in the markets, I sought to profit from them. I worked with patience and without excessive greed and, either astutely or through good fortune, for there was no way to distinguish between the two, gained an income I could subsist on before I started my first full-time job. I simultaneously marvelled at the absurdity and the magnificence of this situation. It typified the kind of zero-sum, freeloading activity that half of the population earned a living from, at the expense of the other half: advertising, law, marketing, finance, management and the rest. For each of my successful trades, there was someone at the other end who was losing out and no doubt having their money managed by some moron with cufflinks who charged them for the privilege.

I began to talk with girls. I would look for those in whom I could see all the infinite depth of a universe in their gaze. Those that, like me, knew the secret that life was simply a game, albeit one of seriousness. I would talk to them only with the eyes at first, sometimes for weeks. If we then spoke it would be like we knew each other. I met several funny, magical girls this way. With each successive step in this new world my confidence grew, and at last I was living my life well.

~~~~~

My desire to know how the world and the living beings in it worked had led me to study the life sciences. Afterwards, I wanted to build things, but our ever-vaunted human technology was still light years away from being able to engineer anything so mysterious as the simplest insect or flower. So I went to work in software engineering, a comparatively simple and logical pursuit, constructing those unglamorous, underappreciated and invisible works of art that put the world at our fingertips, keep planes from colliding in the sky and allow us to escape into alternate realities.

It fascinated me that something as intangible as a software program, something that didn't even really exist, other than in the arrangement of electrons in a wafer of silicon, could exert such an influence over our reality. These creations were the modern day spirits that governed our world, though instead of overseeing us like divinities from mountaintops in the clouds, they ruled as daemons, unblinkingly, in dark basements and data centres.

In a way, Mother Earth herself was a programmer, keeping her algorithms backed up in self-replicating sequences of DNA and patterns of synapses. This thought, that the construction of programs was something inherent in nature, made me feel better about myself in those moments when I found my mind ebbing and my soul dying at work, in front of a computer.

There was a certain beauty to this work. The act of modelling and representing aspects of the world in software systems required the engineer to capture the essence of the entities that they were describing, to identify their indispensable properties and behaviours. There was something of Plato in it. I strove to construct ideal worlds populated by ideal bodies, governed by immutable, ideal rules.

The ideal worlds of my software had their value. The problem was that they were no substitute for the real world, and I often yearned to escape. I worked contracts, spending the intervening times journeying alone or with my friends, Joe, Neil and Red, to discover different corners of the globe. The places we visited were always richer and always more intricate than one could imagine. I loved to find out about the world, the good and the bad, in this way. For me, observing things with my own eyes was the only way. My wanderlust was also a wonderlust. Whenever one of us planned a trip, the others would usually make it, and I would make things work so that I could go away somewhere at least once a year. It kept the inner beast happy.

There was a time when I felt I had reached a good balance between gainful employment and wandering and wondering. Of late, though, I had struggled to motivate myself to work against the backdrop of a globe in which I had witnessed so much that was broken. I could no longer give myself a satisfactory answer to that most fundamental question, *"Why am I doing this?"* It was a criterion I applied to most things in my life. It sounded simplistic, but I was always surprised how easy it was to overcomplicate matters to the point where simple questions and truths were overlooked.

The unavoidable conclusion was that there was no use in working, in the conventional sense, any more. The world was dying, and I was merely abetting the premature demise of our living planet by being complicit in a *programme* that guaranteed that outcome. To those who understood, the enormous methane belches from the East Siberian Sea and from the tundra, now pock-marked with deep craters from spontaneous gas explosions, meant that the world as we knew it did not have long left. For those who did not, or chose not, to understand, life could still continue with a semblance of normality. These were the people who still conscientiously put their recycling into the green boxes outside their houses each week, pretending to themselves that they were making a difference and that everything would be OK. They were the people that still believed the empty words of the politicians, those masters of speaking without actually saying anything, who launched token green initiatives with one hand while signing environmental death warrants with the other. You had to laugh at their childlike naïveté, or you would cry.

The human race had reached what psychologists would identify as the 'bargaining' phase, in the face of our impending demise. There were, though, classifiable groups of people representing each of the five stages of grief: denial, anger, bargaining, depression, acceptance. The bargainers had faith that we could mitigate our grim destiny with green boxes and electric vehicles, but the laws of nature did not cut deals, and I had fallen into the 'acceptance' demographic a long while back. The Arctic methane eruptions were my own turning point, but it could equally have been any one of a number of recent phenomena. Island nations and cities, including downtown Miami, had been abandoned to rising waters. Warm tropical seas had stratified and died in the heat, and were now anoxic, populated only by brightly coloured, toxic algae. Malaria and dengue fever were now endemic in much of continental Europe and diseases thought to be long extinct resurfaced as they slowly re-awoke from thawing permafrost. Across the world, vehicles and buildings spontaneously combusted in heat waves of ferocious intensity that killed people in their tens of thousands.

Greenland had taken a lot of people by surprise. Beneath its ice cap lay not a giant land mass but a ring of islands around a central sea. This had allowed a warmer, higher ocean to push its way deep beneath the two-mile-high cap and to melt it from the base upwards. It was rotting from the inside and had entered a state of collapse, losing thousands of cubic kilometres of ice annually, and gargantuan melt outbursts with accompanying tsunamis were now fairly frequent. One such event had inundated

Reykjavik, though on that occasion a stroke of ill luck in the form of a sub-glacial volcano had been the trigger. Some even attributed the volcano to global heating, pointing out that so much ice mass had been lost from the Greenland cap that the planetary crust had started to rebound, causing elevated seismic activity. Either way, the ice loss was of epic proportions. When central London, Shanghai and New York went the way of Miami, which would not be so long, maybe people would finally sit up and take notice.

Nearly everybody was guilty of contributing to the current parlous situation to a certain degree, not least myself. I was a part of the problem rather than a part of the solution. But the problem now was that there *was* no solution. As with death itself, the outcome was an inevitability. As with death itself, we wilfully blinded ourselves to it. The ones who had been given the power to make a genuine difference, in this struggle that demanded of us a systematic and global response, were those at the top. At their fake environmental summits, when there had still been enough time, they had been presented with a chance. But they had chosen not to take it, electing instead to cut deals with their great chums in Oil & Gas and the Investment Banks, to allow the tar, coal, gas, lignite and crude oil to continue being scraped and pumped from the Earth's crust and ignited in our delicate atmosphere, and to trade in our blue planet for some money. With their greed, they had recklessly chosen to perform a vast, fossil-fuelled, uncontrolled, planetary-scale geo-engineering experiment on the only world we knew.

The ship was sinking – the hour was too late to save it. A lot of people were already going with it. It killed me to see what was happening, and to be so helpless to stop it. At the same time I was gripped with a lewd fascination as I watched the planetary-scale collapse unfold in slow motion.

And thus, my decision to finally quit the *programme*. I would be happier this way. As I knew from Robinson, I could not become unhappy when the *programme* went wrong if I was not a part of it. Aside from this, the *programme* had started to disgust me. It, and the world, were governed by people like Miles Warren M.B.A, sallow money-wraiths who were now well out of their depth and struggling to pretend that they weren't. The northern latitudes blazed, indignant youth rioted, super-storms smashed whole cities, wars erupted over resources and the population grew by two million people every week. All the while, these plausible-sounding, suited clowns would appear on TV, nod knowingly, and spew forth on such matters in specious and reassuring platitudes, using laboured gesticulations for emphasis, like mime artists with sound. As with the words of my grandmother, their words were perilously misleading to the unwary. Unlike my grandmother, they didn't even mean well.

V

Tina had been asleep when I got back to the pousada. I had silently lain awake for a long time in the night turning things over in my head, making plans, the *mzungu* I was. It was the curse of having burst our erstwhile bubble of ignorant bliss. She was still sleeping when I arose early. She was a good sleeper. I could only sleep as well as her in dark winters, like those at home.

Donning shorts, a singlet and flipflops, I crept out, not wishing to incur the displeasure unbridled on those that disturbed her slumber. I followed the track that led to the deserted *praia grande*, ran the length of the beach and back in bare feet by the water's edge, did fifty push-ups and bathed in the sea. I lay in the breeze to dry off and inspected one of the strange and intricate sand-dollar shells that were common on the beaches here. Each and every one looked as though someone had painstakingly etched a picture of a flower onto it. Perhaps it had fallen from a mermaid's purse, it occurred to me. It was commonplace to see these scarab-like shark egg casings on the beach as well. Sand dollars and mermaids' purses, ha. I was disappointed that Tina wasn't there to share the moment with.

When mostly dry, I returned to the village to call Joe from one of the boxes on the sandy tracks that were the thoroughfares. I wanted to hear directly what was happening at home. I tapped in his number, which I had memorised along with the handful of others I considered essential.

I knew Joe from university, where we had both belonged to the boxing club - I a light-heavy and he a heavyweight, a 6' 4", 17-stone unit. We had sparred regularly but never fought in earnest. As chance had it, we both ended up living in the small Somerset city of Bath some years later. It was the city where Joe had grown up.

Joe was one of those rarely encountered people who live by their convictions without compromise. He had studied philosophy, but had dropped out in his final year after arguing with his tutors. He had contested that animal sixth senses - the ways in which creatures often seem to know things without any apparent means of knowing - were evidence of channels of communication that were, as yet, barely known to us. He considered these channels to be comparable in sophistication to human languages. His tutors had ridiculed his arguments and his dissertation on the subject. Disillusioned by what he saw as narrow-mindedness in what should have been the most enlightened of disciplines, he walked away from the course, just weeks before his final exams. I still remember his words from that time: "Anybody can be a philosopher, you don't need a *degree* in it, you just need to be able to see the truth and tell the truth. That's all a philosopher is — a truth-teller. You have to be able to see through all the illusions we build around ourselves. The strange thing is that, when they hear the truth, often people won't understand it, or won't want to listen to it. They'll choose the illusion instead."

Joe now worked doing anything honourable, as he put it, a stance that ruled out a good number of professions in his view. He mostly taught private classes, but also blogged, gave lectures and had a handful of unfinished books on the go, as well as one that he had published, a book about local folkloric characters for children. He was clear blue-eyed, wore his tawny hair long, often in a ponytail, and had a compass tattooed on the outside of one formidable bicep. I had never asked why. He'd explain it one day if he wanted to. A failed relationship some years back had left him broken-hearted and embittered against the fairer sex for a while, and his humour to this day was seasoned with a dash of self-parody from that time.

"Hello?" came an unhurried voice from the other end of the line.

"Alright buster, it's Joss. How is it?"

"You ask a lot of questions," came back the reply. I was reassured by his usual insouciance. He followed up with a laugh to himself. "Yeah, it's alright, have you been watching the stuff on the news?"

"I have. I wondered if it had hit the West Country yet?" I said, asking after our home.

He took pause for thought before replying, or perhaps it was the delay on the line. The voice was unchanged when it came. "Kind of, there's less in the shops and it's hard to get petrol, but I think it's worse in other places. I've had classes cancelled, a lot of people are staying at home."

Disappointing. "That's a bit boring," I yawned, "From the telly it looked like complete carnage. I thought you might have at least put on a balaclava and punched a plod in the face. I would've done if I was there. What are you planning to do, anyway? Anything?"

"Well, luckily I've got a holiday booked the week after next with Nyree in Italy so we're at least getting out of the country. If it wasn't for that it would be difficult, all the flights are full, it's holiday time as it is. After that, dunno mate, I'll see. Neil's seeing this new girl, Frederica, who's Italian, and she's invited us all out to a country house her family has there, that's why we're going, so I suppose we could stay there if we had to."

"Italian girlfriend? Better hope she doesn't have any brothers or he'll be sleeping with the fishes if it goes like it did with the last one," I smiled. Neil's romantic life was never dull, and was the source of great entertainment to the rest of us.

"Hm. I don't know if you could call her a girlfriend, she hasn't started ear-bashing him yet so it's not really a proper relationship. They're still at the stage where they actually like each other."

"Does that happen?" I feigned seriousness.

"It can happen," Joe stated authoritatively.

"Talking of such things, how's Ny doing?" I changed the subject. Nyree was a half-Israeli Kiwi, Joe's finer half of many years. She was an ethereal and gentle soul who, against all odds, loved Joe and his idiosyncrasies, enduring his frequent outspoken and mock-misogynistic monologues with an air of patient resignation and the faintest hint of a smirk.

"Nyree?" Joe seemed surprised I had asked. "Yeah she's, uhh, still ruining my life."

"Oh," I offered my condolences, laughing inside. Of

all the band of misfits that were my friends, Joe was the most mis-fit.

"Listen, what I called for…" I continued, "tell me what you think of this for an idea. I've come up with the notion of going down to Patagonia while all the chaos blows over back home, get a cabin and fix it up or something. If it doesn't blow over and it all goes belly-up, it's not a bad place to be either. There's hardly anyone down there, plenty of water if we're near the mountains, fishing…"

"Yeah, OK, that sounds good," Joe interrupted, sounding far-off.

I was a little taken aback. "How do you mean?"

Joe could be relied upon to take the bigger picture into account. "Yeah I'll come, it sounds good. There's no reason why it won't all go tits-up, it happens to all civilizations. This one is basically a giant Ponzi scheme that's guaranteed to fail. I was planning to live the life of a barbarian in the Apennines if we couldn't go back home - they've got bears there - but Patagonia sounds better. What do we eat there, llama?"

"Mostly fish."

"I'm talking about meat."

I thought back to the time, years previously, when I'd travelled there to learn Spanish and walk in the Fitzroy Mountains. "Oh, then guanaco, they're like llama. And ñandu, if you can catch them, they're like small ostriches."

"OK, deal," Joe concluded, seemingly satisfied with my answer.

I waited, but there was no more comment.

"Right, that worked out more easily than I expected. Just a few minor details to sort, then," I joked. "Are you serious about this mate?"

Joe murmured agreement, he sounded more serious this time. "Yeah, I don't want to be left here fighting off hordes of marauding peasants if it gets really bad, people are starting to act like village idiots, the usual stuff, you know. The plods scare me more than anyone - they're the biggest psychopaths of all. They're out in their bell-end hats locking up people who've insulted them on the internet, along with people they don't like the look of. It'll be good to get away for a bit. I don't even really like it here at the moment. Joining up with you guys will be a good trip apart from anything else, communing with nature and all that. I'll just sort my stuff and speak to Nyree."

This surprised me. I had never heard Joe say he was scared of anything. The rest of what he said mirrored what I had started to feel before we left: that our home was no longer really our home.

"And Neil?" I asked.

Joe's usual humorous tone returned. "Yeah, I'm not sure about him, he's besotted with this Italian girl and not thinking rationally. It's like a mental illness. I'll have to check. I'll call you in a few days."

I cursed myself as I realised how difficult I would be to contact. "Sorry, chief, I'm off the grid at the moment. I don't have a phone."

This elicited a sigh of disdain, "Riiiiighhhht…." It was followed by an expectant pause.

"I'll get a phone."

"Yes. Welcome to the 20th century. Oh, hang on, it's

the 21st," Joe mocked. I took it graciously. He continued, "Text me your number when you've got it. I'll try calling Redface too, we can make a grand tour of it."

"Plan," I concurred, "I'm not sure what Red's up to out there in Korea, I tried emailing him but it's a waste of electrons, he never replies. I don't know if he even reads them. Come to that, I don't even know if he can read." Joe chuckled at this.

Thinking sensibly again, I reflected to see if there was anything we'd omitted to discuss. I didn't think there was.

"Right then, good times. Apart from the world being on fire and the imminent collapse of civilization and everything."

"Could be worse," postulated Joe. "My chick could be nagging me to get off the phone. Oh, she is. Forgive me, I've got to go and engage in non-transcendental conversation relating to housework, by the looks of things. Cheers for now."

I could hear Nyree protesting in the background and yelling her greetings to me. I gave farewells and yelled back before the line went quiet, then hung up the handset. I felt light-headed from the exercise and lack of breakfast, but enjoyed the sensation, experiencing the heightened sense of alertness that came with the hunger.

VI

I walked back to the pousada, where Tina was eating a melon she had bought for breakfast.

"Oh, there you are! Where were you? I ate your half of the melon, there's none left for you," she beamed, savouring the situation.

"That's a bummer, I'm hungry. I was speaking with Joe. How about you?"

Tina had spoken with her mother the previous evening and was concerned for her. We talked about things back home and exchanged the disjointed fragments of information we had picked up. Her mother, in London, had described a military presence on the streets. I asked her what she wanted to do and she said she'd like to stay where we were, it would have to settle down at home before long.

I prepared myself for what I was going to say to her, then said it. "Listen, what do you think of this, babe? Joe, Nyree, Neil and Neil's girlfriend, Frederica, are going to

Italy on holiday."

Tina was looking at me suspiciously, but smiled at the mention of Frederica. "Neil's got a new girlfriend?"

"More or less, yes," I said, a corner of my mouth turning up in a half-smile as I remembered Joe's comment about the ear-bashing. "Anyway... Joe thinks it'll probably get worse before it gets better and reckons they mightn't go back home for a while. That's to say, they may come out here and meet up with us."

Tina stiffened as I spoke, but I carried on.

"The idea is, if it came to the worst and there was a lot of trouble at home and everywhere else, we could go to Patagonia to sit it out, it's quiet down there."

"So, you and Joe have just gone and totally changed our plans without even asking me?" she remonstrated, beginning to get upset. "I can't believe you've done that." Tears were in her eyes.

I attempted to explain myself better. "It's just an idea, lovely. Nothing's fixed for definite. That's why I wanted to talk it over with you now. I... I've got a bad gut feeling about going further north at the moment, that's all. When it's the right time we'll see Marajó, no matter what. Don't worry."

In the north-east corner of the country, on the equator and a world away from Patagonia, lay the island of Marajó, the place of Tina's father's birth, and one that had acquired a mystical significance for her. The understanding between us was that it would be a focal point for our travels in Brazil.

My words fell on ears of stone. "If it's so important for you to go to Patagonia with your friends instead of doing what we've dreamed of for years together, that's fine," Tina fired emotionally. "I'll go home, I don't want to leave my Mum on her own." Now she was crying.

I felt like I'd been kicked in the balls and slammed back against a wall. She pushed me away when I tried to embrace her and asked me to leave her on her own. Reluctantly, I left. I walked aimlessly around the village for a time, reflecting on what I should have done differently. It would be easy to ignore everything and carry on up the coast, and Tina would be happy that way, but something primeval from within me told me that we had to get away from people to somewhere quiet. I hated to ignore these signals, which were nearly always more accurate than any amount of reasoned thinking.

~~~~~

I ended up back at the internet shack. I had no appetite, though I was now feeling dizzy from not eating, on top of the tremendous regret I felt from how things had gone earlier. I asked the kid at the door, who was just opening it up, for a machine, and he powered one up for me. The computer, an old model, seemed to groan to a start. I stared at the screen, waiting for it to come to life and distract me from my own thoughts.

Once online, I spent hours and lost myself searching for reasons why my gut might be telling me to turn around and go south but just found more of the same news as before. Whole towns burned and abandoned in Siberia and Canada, with some saying the wildfires would burn for years, right through the winters. These fires were large enough to burn the earth itself and create their own weather — massive electrical firestorms of pyrocumulonimbus clouds. The jet stream carried their smoke for thousands of miles, turning the skies a cloudless grey in London, New York and San Francisco. People tried to live and work as usual in England while looters and vigilantes ran wild. When my eyes started to hurt I sat and looked at the football poster on the wooden wall in front of me, resting them and allowing my mind to be still.

There was a tap on my shoulder, I turned my head and almost lost balance from faintness. It was Tina. Her face looked reconciliatory. "Hey, space cadet. You've been here for hours," she said. "C'mon, let's get some lunch."

I settled with the boy on the door and we walked to a place nearby with tables on a veranda shaded by lemon trees. We took a bench and saw a hummingbird with iridescent wings flit into view across the track and take a minute sip from a flowering tree before vanishing again.

Over a lime juice, Tina opened up. Strains of *forró* music reached us from inside the café. "I spoke with my Mum again and told her what you said to me about going to Patagonia," she said. I nodded. "She agreed that you were wrong in the way you put your suggestion to me, but she thought that, with the way things are, it would be better for me to stay with you. She also thought that going to Patagonia wasn't a bad idea, she thinks we've seen the best part of Brazil. She remembers going around the country with my father, and even back then she said the southern provinces had much lower crime and she received far less bother than in the other regions. My brother's going to go back to London to be with her." She looked at me and I felt the air between us clear.

I drew breath. "Sorry about hitting you with it like that, I suppose I could have introduced it a bit more gently. We'll still get up to Marajó one day, I promise. Maybe the general hassle up that way is why I've got that bad feeling. *You'd* get a lot of attention for sure, looking like you do. Apart from that, everything's so *broken* at the moment, it feels like. It doesn't seem that it would take much to nudge things over the edge, even here. I'd prefer to be somewhere away from people, *properly* away from people, for a bit. So… we're on then?"

Tina looked at me without a flicker in her gaze. "When is stoopid Joe arriving then?" she said, breaking into a laugh. She laughed harder when I told her of the mockery I had endured at the hands of Joe for not having a phone. "Nice one, mister I-don't-speak-to-anyone-any-more-because-I've-got-email!" she joked in a caricatured impression of me.

"This is worse than being with my mates. Maybe you should go back home!" I riposted, setting her up.

She didn't hesitate. "Fine, I will. Have fun in Patagonia with Joe and the nandoolies or whatever they're called."

"Ñandu!" I corrected her. "I love you, T."

"Aw, that's nice," she teased. The spark was back in her eyes.

~~~~~

We had met on the web three years previously. Even in her photograph her eyes of jet black had betrayed the pure spirit that lay behind them and had me mesmerised. Although clearly unattainable, I had redacted a message one solitary evening over a beer and a home-brew curry and sent it to her for the hell of it. This, after permitting myself an extraordinary exemption, in this instance, to my law of never associating with lawyers.

The gods had been smiling on me. She liked the way I had written to her, a change from the advances of cash-rich, time-poor, prematurely aged city boys, or the chat from deprived and depraved squaddies stationed in far-off hell-holes, she explained. We began a long correspondence. When we met for the first time, I lost my breath and it was all I could do to hold myself together and talk. We had been for a drink and wandered around the crowded Christmas market in Bath, the streets lit up above us.

The deal-clincher, maybe, was when I made her my *chermoula* with pangasius and flatbread. She had gasped involuntarily at the first mouthful, the combination of fresh coriander, flat-leaf parsley, lime juice, fresh ginger, sea salt, mint, lime leaves, chilli, fresh garlic, capers, pepper and olive oil overwhelming her senses, in a good way, as I had hoped it would. I still remember the way she looked at me.

I had ridden the wave since then, not questioning how it was that we grew to spend all our time together and then to love each other, just going with it, with the unknown, and with her capricious, argumentative nature. Never looking too far ahead. We kissed.

VII

"We're on here, pal. Tina's cool with the plan. What about your end?" Two days had passed. From where I stood, in the garden of the pousada, I looked around to check that nobody could see me. I had obtained a pink sparkling phone the day before from a girl on the island who was taking the boat to Paranaguá to get a new one.

"Don't tell me she agreed just like that? She must have broken your balls at least a bit?" Joe interrogated.

"OK, there were some waterworks, and then she had to talk with her mum, but then it was cool," I confessed.

"Obviously," Joe pronounced sagely. "Yeah, Nyree's on board, Neil's working on Freddie. Frederica, that is. I think he's trying to sell it to her as a romantic getaway. I've looked at flights, there are still some from Rome to Buenos Aires, not too exorbitant either. By the way, I spoke to Red, I don't think he'll come, he's made some similar plans of his own but reckons he'll go to Canada with Jen, he's fed up with the Norks threatening to kick off."

"Oh, that's a downer." I screwed up my nose. It was a shame they couldn't make it. Jen, Red's wife, was a quiet, softly spoken Mongolian girl who had been brought up in a yak herding family before a devastating Winter *dzud* had killed most of their herd, driving them to move to Ulán Bator. Finding the cramped life in the tented *ger* districts of the capital unbearable, they had returned to herding with the help of extended family. Not wanting to step backwards, Jen had carved her own path and made her way to Seoul, home to the world's largest Mongolian expatriate community. She spoke little of this time of her life. In the Korean capital, she had forged a life for herself as a singer and had met Red as he taught her English. Within a year they had married, admiring each other's resilience, humour and independence of spirit.

I asked Joe the question that was hanging over us. "So, shall we push the button then? If you get those flights we'll do a U-ey here and head back down to BA."

Joe didn't ponder his reply. "Let's do it. I'll get four tickets while I still can. I'll text you when it's done."

A buzz of electricity passed silently over me from my crown to the soles of my feet. "Good skills, I'll get some transport sorted for us. We met a crazy Aussie on the way up through Brazil who was doing up camper vans, he should be able to sort us out."

"Good, let me know if there's anything we need to bring. Med kit or tools or anything you can't get out there," Joe said.

I thought for a moment. "Medical kit, we'll be alright, you can get anything you want from the pharmacy out here, they're like the doctor's. Electronics are what you can't get without bankrupting yourself. GPS, solar chargers, satellite internet hotspot, a tablet or something to get on the internet with. If we're out in the sticks, it'll be the only way of knowing what's happening in the rest of the world. Plus, while you can download stuff, get any info you can find on surviving outdoors, it can't hurt to have as much as possible." I thought some more. "Oh, plus tents and camping gear. That should be it."

Joe signed off calmly. "Alright. I'll see what I can do."

VIII

Tina and I were on the small ferry off the island early the next morning. I had already received a message from Joe: *Flights booked. Neil & Freddie are in. Neil still sick in the head. Arrive in 3 weeks. Good luck with getting the van.*

Amid the noise and the fumes from the boat's outboard engines, we spotted our last groups of dolphins and watched the Ilha do Mel, the Isle of Honey, recede into the distance. We threaded our way through the sandbanks that had been brought near the surface by the low tide. Tina clasped my hand as we rocked on the small waves. It had been a special place. With a sense of purpose but no rush, we disembarked at Paranaguá and took the first *colectivo* bus back to Curitiba. It was packed and noisy with the animated conversations of locals, of which we could understand very little. It contrasted starkly with the outward trip to the Ilha. Starting from Curitiba, we had taken the old train that descends through the forested *Serra do Mar*, the Mountains of the Sea, atop which the city sits. Crossing precarious bridges that sat astride ravines amid towering rocky peaks, we had glimpsed some of the secrets of the Atlantic rainforest. There are dazzling, metallic blue butterflies the size of frisbees that fly like flatfish swim. Giant spider webs like radio antennae are slung between creepers. Then, there are huge, buttressed trees dripping with bromeliads, heliconia and orchids that serve as provisioning stops for hummingbirds. Parrots float between treetops and eagles soar overhead. This was just what we could see from our seats on the railway carriage, and I marvelled to think of what lay deeper in the forest.

From where we sat now, on a dirty bus on a dismal autoroute, mindlessly cheerful samba music blaring from the speakers, there were no hints as to the wonders that lay just over the skyline. I felt animated to know of what was there, but this came laced with melancholy to think of the millions of similarly hidden miracles we must have passed by, oblivious, in our lives. This kind of beauty was undervalued in our time. Nature was being reduced to something that could be visited in reserves and parks, where you would be charged for the privilege of seeing it. Outside of these sanctuaries it was dying, being blown away with disregard like dandelion seeds, cuckoo spit and the silken strands of cobwebs. Streams gave way to highways with rivers of heavy trucks, leaf litter to plastic detritus, wooded glades to cities full of advertising hoardings, meadows to lifeless tracts of monoculture, brush to barbed wire fences, plains to soulless airports, birds to planes, animals to obese, angry, tailgating motorists. Yet, amongst all this, you would sometimes encounter something magical, unexpectedly, from nowhere, appearing against all the odds like an inhabited planet emerging from the void of deep space. It could be as simple as the splash of fire of a cluster of poppies on a railway siding, or as mysterious as a flotilla of by-the-wind sailors washed up on a beach. No matter where you are, never allow your sense of wonder to die, nor ever stop looking - the miraculous is always close by.

LUKE F. D. MARSDEN

~~~~~

That I retained my sense of wonder into adulthood I owed in great measure to a house spider. This is the true tale of the once and fearless spider:

Mopping the floor of my small kitchen in Bath one morning, I took the two front legs, on the left side, off a spider that was hidden in a crack beneath a skirting board. It emerged, crippled by the injury and the bleach solution, and ran to another dark corner where it disappeared. I cursed to myself and apologised to the spider, I hated to damage them, but, as is the way, I soon forgot the incident. The next morning I sat alone eating breakfast at my table. As I ate and prepared for the day, the spider appeared at the far corner of the table and rushed across the surface towards me. It stopped in the centre and raised its two good front legs on the right side high, in a gesture of seeming defiance, or perhaps simply in an attempt to communicate. In any case, at that moment it died right in front of me, in the defiant, or greeting, posture. It was so impossibly beyond what I would attribute to a spider that I never told anyone, not even Tina. It wasn't worth it.

I never forgot what I learned in that moment: to be humble, to be honest with myself, to see things as they really are, and to live without fear. I cannot explain why I took these lessons from this occurrence, but I did. It was as if the spider had delivered a message to me. I carried its image around in my mind, indelibly marked there like a cerebral tattoo. It had yanked me back to my senses on the many occasions when the petty concerns of everyday life had seemed daunting.

~~~~~

After the haul of the boat and bus journeys, we spent two nights in Curitiba and then travelled to Florianopolis, and the Ilha de Santa Catarina, on which half of this picturesque city resides. We were there to meet a man, although this word did not do him sufficient justice, named Kay McBean. A long-haired, drunken Australian with the air of an aging rocker, he had lived a mysterious existence for the previous seven years in the former fishing village of Campeche, fixing up camper vans at his own leisurely pace and "helping out", as he put it, performing small acts of kindness that went unnoticed to all but those touched by them. He had helped us out the first time we had arrived at this place. Campeche sprawls along the handsome *praia do Campeche* beach for several kilometres. We had got off the bus at the wrong end of the village, and, obviously disoriented, Kay had offered us a ride to our pousada in his prototype drop-top Kombi camper van. He was half-cut, so I drove, and he had told us of his life along the way. Over the following two weeks he had taken time to show us his favourite parts of the island, with its lagoons, hills, villages and beaches.

This time, knowing our way, we got off the bus at the end of the line in Campeche and walked to the local store, where they would know of Kay's whereabouts. We were informed that we could find him in his workshop and we continued the couple of quiet, sand-dusted blocks to where a lot with a makeshift garage and a transparent, corrugated plastic roof formed his centre of operations. Two brightly painted Kombis were lined up against a wall of breezeblocks. Another with a hole cut in the roof was in the centre of the workshop floor. Kay, in a dusty vest and shorts, was alongside it bending lengths of metal tubing with a blowtorch. We walked in off the road. He looked up, gave us a huge, craggy grin, put down his torch and picked up an open bottle of beer, taking a long draught.

"Look, guys, she's another drop-top. Oy've sold two of 'em. It's happenin'!" He walked up and gave Tina a strong hug, "You look beautiful, love," followed by me.

"Wot's with yerz, anyway? Wozn't expecting yerz turning up here unannounced. Not that yerz're not welcome, of course! Yerz look good kids!"

"Looking good yourself mate, have you been pumping iron?" I kidded, alluding to his wiry frame. "Here, I brought you this, a little late, but it's to say thanks for last time." I passed him a patterned seashell we had found on a beach on the island. "It's from the Ilha do Mel. When you find yourself a new woman, take her up there. I'll be jealous when you do!"

Kay had hit the bottle when his girlfriend, a local, had left him. There was a faint sadness behind his great energy.

He took the seashell and looked at us, genuinely moved. "Yerz didn't need to do that, guys!" He slipped the shell into his pocket then straightened himself to his full height, taller than my six feet two, and fixed his gaze into the distance. "Listen, blow this, we need to go an' have a proper catch-up. Let's go, c'mon, let's go."

He strode purposefully out of the workshop, leaving everything as it stood. We bought beers from the store, walked the few hundred yards to the beach and sat in the shade of a parasol, exchanging news and stories. I told Kay of our decision to turn around and head south, and of our wish to buy one of his Kombis for the journey.

"Bloody brilliant idea mayte, Oy'd come with yerz if Oy wasn't so attached to this place, she's moy home now. Don't blame yerz wantin' to get away from folks fer a whoile. People as a whole are a great bunch of silly buggers in the grand scheme, even though yerz get a lot of bloody brilliant ones. The planet's all goin' to hell. Koynda maykes me glad Oy never had kids. Oy'd feel sorry fer the little bloighters. Dunno wot they'd do with the'selves in this new world, she's not the same world we knew growin' up. Anythin' yerz wanna do now there's a million other blokes've got there before yerz. Still, Oy've had a good loife. With luck, it'll be a whoile before any trouble reaches this place and a long time 'fore it hits Pata-gonia. The food proices'll be wot duz it in the end. The old *flyin' rivers* that used to come off the forest have stopped comin', there's not enough forest left an' they've droied up. Not enough rain anymore fer the food we need. Not long before there's big trouble. Let's see if Oy'm still around boy then. With oil bein' expensive and all that as well, we're bloody lucky all our vehicles run on *alcohol*, bit loike me. Those Kombis back there'll run just as well on alcohol or petrol, *flex-fuel engine*. Alcohol or petrol, it's the Brazilian way, they run their cars on the same bloody stuff they drink in their *caipirinhas*, and that's never gonna run out!" He took a great draught from the beer next to him, then turned to us. "Oy'll tell yerz wot Oy'm gonna do, Oy'm gonna *give* yerz a Kombi, yerz can help me build her."

"Whoa, Kay, come on, we'll pay you for it, that's not a problem," I responded, astounded by his generous offer.

"Listen, mayte. Oy'm bloody rich. Oy'm tellin' yerz – Oy'm bloody rich. This Kombi thing is a hobby, Oy loyke it. If yerz'll help me, we'll build one up for yer trip dahn south just the way yerz wannit. It'll be a laugh, what d'yerz say?"

I looked at Tina and back at Kay. "We're not going to turn down an offer like that, mate. Kay, you are *gente boa*, good people!" I raised my bottle.

"Cheers you beauties!" He raised his bottle and we cheers-ed our new enterprise. When the sun went down, we lit a fire of driftwood on the beach and shot the breeze and drank beers late into the warm night. Kay had found his place here - I envied him that. Some day the wandering would stop, I told myself, when you have found your place.

IX

The two weeks spent building the Kombi passed in a haze of hungover early morning starts with the sunrise, laughter and hard work. We worked on the van that had been in progress when we arrived. Kay was an early riser and a grafter when he wasn't distracted by the frequent visits from the surfers, skateboarders and drifters whom he had made his friends here. He never seemed drunk, although he drank beers from dawn to way beyond dusk. "Can't operate properly without 'em," he stated factually.

I ended up doing most of the work, other than finishing the drop-top, under instruction and supervision from Kay: "Yerz're gonna have to know how the bloody thing works fer when she breaks dahn. She needs a bloke ter look after her. She's not gonna look after her*self*."

I raised the suspension, put on new wheels for the gravel and dirt roads we would encounter and fitted out the back, putting in folding upper bunks and storage compartments under bench seats that doubled as lower bunks. Between these, wooden panels could be slotted, turning the lower bunks into one big bed with more storage beneath. Tina helped speed up the operation, making runs with lists of parts to the auto-repair shop, keeping us watered and fed, and maintaining our spirits with her presence and mechanic-inspired attire of dungarees with bikini top. To finish the job, she and one of Kay's graffiti artist acquaintances, a dreadlocked girl named Billie, painted the entire van with a scene of the Ilha de Santa Catarina. There was a long beach with surfers and kite surfers riding the crashing waves, the small Ilha do Campeche in the background and seabirds swooping in the foreground. It was a masterpiece.

"To remind you of us and this place," said Billie.

"We'll call her Little Billie," I replied, and an impromptu christening ceremony was performed, Billie painting the name on the van and Kay smashing a bottle of beer over the roof with more force than necessary, provoking much laughter. He then launched into a speech.

"To Tina and Joss, good maytes, good people, and happy. There's no logic to wot maykes yer happy, yer just are or y'aren't. Here's to their trip dahn south, Pata-gonia way. It's a bloody good idea if yerz ask me, and here's to the Billie-wagon gettin' them dahn there. She's a beauty of a Kombi – best yet. Whatever yerz're lookin' for, I hope yerz find it. Yerz moight've never lost it! And now we're gonna have a bloody big party. Cheers."

~~~~~

Tina and I disappeared to get supplies for the festivities, which would be our leaving bash.

"I'd like to stay here some more time, it seems a shame to be leaving," Tina dropped into the conversation on the way to the store, voicing my own sentiment.

I squeezed her hand. "I know, lovely, but Joe and all

the others are going to be arriving in Argentina in about a week. If we leave it much longer, we'll be pushing it to get down there on time."

"Okay my *mzungu*!" Tina smirked, before skipping ahead and launching into an impression of me she was working on involving checking watches, calendars and diaries, scratching my head and tapping numbers into calculators, and muttering to myself about deadlines and obligations. It was very funny but I soaked it up, trying not to betray any type of amusement. When she was done laughing at her own performance, out of breath and still smirking to herself, she picked back up the thread of discussion. "How are they getting on in Italy anyway?"

"Not bad at all." I had received a couple of updates from Joe. "Freddie's parents' place is amazing, apparently, they must be minted. Joe and Nyree are getting on well with her too, I don't think they knew her that well before. They've been out on scooters, exploring the villages around where they're staying, going walking and cooking up nice meals in the evenings, all with plenty of the local wine. Sounds like happy days."

"There's no trouble around there then?" Tina questioned.

"Joe hasn't mentioned it. He did say it was lucky he got the tickets when he did though, they're all gone now. Seems like we're not the only ones going to Argentina. Judging from the news, though, everything's pretty messed up."

I had snatched a few brief moments on the web on Kay's computer in breaks from the work on Little Billie. Same old. Riots, plod crackdowns, sabotage, curfews, hacking, general chaos, it wasn't showing any signs of subsiding. The Mediterranean countries were getting in on the action as well, the indignant long-term unemployed youth there deciding they had nothing to lose either and emulating their British cousins with enthusiasm. It appeared that these millions of mostly bright, educated and motivated young people were just not needed, or even valued, by the countries they lived in. For many of those whose sense of wellbeing derived from feeling valued by others it had become a problem that was spilling over. They were learning to value themselves instead.

~~~~~

We walked back from the store, to Kay's place, laden down with meat, fish, bread, beer and charcoal. There were no signs here of local people stockpiling. The shelves were still full and the service cheerful.

When we arrived back at the house it was already alive with the vibes of Brazilian reggae and Kay's collection of highly individual friends. We made our way with the bags, clumsily, through the haze of smoke from weed and *kretek* clove cigarettes, and went out through the sliding glass doors into the back yard. There we dropped our provisions next to the brick barbeque, our shoulders and fingers hurting from carrying them. Sweeping the residual ashes from the ash pit into an empty bag, I pulled out a paper sack of charcoal, popped the caps off bottles of beer for Tina and myself, and worked on getting the fire burning.

The barbeque soon became one of the social focal points of the party, and over fire-tending, grilling and eating we talked at length with those we had before met only briefly. In some, I recognised the same sadness that Kay carried with him, an air that they had left something behind that they could never go back to. Others had the undertone of regret that sometimes comes with a life of unadulterated hedonism. Then, there were those that had such an irrepressible life force and zeal for the future that it left me feeling unworthy, with a sense that I had to be more like them. With all of them, I was interested in their take on the events in the destabilised world. Most were from the 'get your kicks while you can' school of thought. All wished us luck.

Later, the night passed too quickly. Tina was exhilarated at having the opportunity to dance. She danced *forró* for hours, learning the nuances of the form with some of the fine exponents who were present at the party. It was impressive to watch her, and them. I had tried to learn to dance, but did not take naturally to it.

For my part, I hung out around the barbeque being entertained by people's stories and telling some of my own. I eventually got speaking with a fellow Brit, who had made numerous visits to request food from the barbeque. He was an enterprising sort, named Dwike, who had been Kay's first customer, buying his first converted Kombi. Dwike had set up a small software operation in Florianopolis, "bringing British quality practices to the Latin American market", as he put it. He was an affable character, unthreatening and rotund, and mingled as easily with the potheads and bohemians at the party as I assumed he did with his business clients.

We talked tech for a while, Dwike informing me of recent advancements in the world of software development and extolling the benefits of a new open source e-commerce platform he had started using for some of his projects. I was surprised at how much I enjoyed this technical discussion, and I found myself hoping that my engineering skills would be of use again one day. I switched the thread of conversation when we had exhausted the subject.

"What do you think about what's happening back

home?" I asked him.

"The trouble? They'll sort it out, they always sort it out," he said, chewing voraciously on a hot dog. "Anyway, doesn't matter to me, I live *here*."

"Hm," I mused. He could be right.

"What about all of the environmental disasters? You know, global heating?" I followed up.

"They'll think of something. They always think of something. They'll put a mirror in space or something," he surmised, squirting mustard onto the third of his hot dog that was left and putting it whole into his mouth before he had swallowed the previous mouthful.

"You have great faith in technology, mate. *Too* much faith, perhaps," I said. "In my view we've missed our chance. We're done for. I spend half my time reading about this stuff, I'm obsessed with it. Here's a fact that may interest you. At thirty five degrees wet-bulb temperature, that's basically thirty five degrees with one hundred percent humidity, a threshold is crossed. It's the point at which humans can no longer cool themselves through sweating, and so lose the ability to control their own body temperature. It's lethal. Just *thirty five degrees*. You can get the same result with a higher temperature and lower humidity. Up until about five years ago, thirty five degrees wet bulb had never been recorded anywhere in the world - surprising but true. It's because most of the world's humid regions are next to the oceans, and so their temperatures tend to get moderated by the water. Since then, though, it's started to become fairly commonplace. A lot of people are starting to die this way in heatwaves, most of them in far-flung places - China and the West Pacific, and Pakistan - that's why you don't hear much about it. It's because of the hotter oceans. The sea regularly heats up to over thirty five degrees in those regions."

"Yeah?" Dwike raised his eyebrows, above the small lenses of his glasses, causing his brow to wrinkle beneath his hairless head. "What about air conditioning?" he joked.

He must have seen my face drop, although I didn't mean it to. I was often left disillusioned by people's unwillingness to engage in sincere discussion on this kind of subject.

"Well, if that's the case," he backtracked, "I suppose we might as well get our kicks while we can."

He took another sausage from the barbeque and stuffed it into another roll, almost simultaneously raising it to his mouth to chew off a bite.

~~~~~

In the morning, Kay awoke us early and gave both Tina and I a hug before he left on some unannounced outing.

"Take care, yerz both. Look after her, mayte. I wanna see yerz both back here sometime. She'll be a'right. And then we'll take the Billie-van up to yer Ilha do Mel, though Oy don't believe it's better'n this place!"

With a final big, craggy grin he was off before we had time to thank him properly, and I felt choked up. I looked over at Tina and she was silently in tears. We lay together for a while and got up and cleaned the place from top to bottom, which also served to sober us up. It didn't feel right to leave a note for Kay, the departing ritual was over. Through Little Billie, his spirit would travel with us.

Around midday, we loaded up Little Billie, jumped in

the front and, with windows down, music playing and a satisfyingly loud judder from the engine, pulled away from the workshop and headed for the centre of Florianopolis, and the bridge over the bay that would take us back to the mainland.

X

We drove down through the terrain that we had covered on the way up from Uruguay. The ocean lay to our left. On our right, rose the green mountains of the Serra Geral, which harboured still-formidable vestiges of what was once all Atlantic rainforest. We stopped in Porto Alegre, the happy port on the immense freshwater *Lagoa dos Patos* lagoon, to restore ourselves with steaks and the dark beer made by the descendants of the German settlers in this region. It was good for the blood.

In the morning, I assembled our medical kit from a friendly pharmacy, buying up their remaining Amoxycillin and Ciprofloxacin antibiotics, Itraconazol antifungal and Metronidazole against amoebic dysentery. To this, I added sterile swabs, bandages, plaster strips, a sewing kit, rehydration salts, ear drops, eye drops, Mercurochrome antiseptic, Iodine tincture for water purification, and ibuprofen. Tina bought industrial amounts of feminine hygiene products, soaps, contraceptives, toothpaste and brushes, alcohol hand gel, cosmetic lotions, oils, deodorants and moisturisers – something I was powerless to argue against.

"We're going to have to go back and ask Kay for another van just for your cosmetics laboratory and toilet rolls," I bantered as we walked back to the Kombi with our purchases. "We'll need one of those big, articulated land trains like they have in Australia that take quarter of a mile to stop when you press the brakes."

"OK, you can stop now," said Tina in monotone, unamused.

"We can call it Giant Bill Greybeard, Little Billie's Granddad," I persisted.

"Well, my van's going to smell damn fine compared to yours," she smiled back.

"Hm, maybe," I mused. "At least you're not as bad as Joe's old girlfriend, Fiona. She wouldn't go anywhere without battery-powered hair straighteners. It was ridiculous. She once brought them trekking in Nepal. Her hair was straight anyway, she didn't even need them."

I realised as soon as the words left my mouth that recounting this tale at this time was a mistake.

Tina went into defensive mode. "Oh, thanks. Please, compare me some more to your friends' dizzy exes. I can't get enough of it."

I attempted to rescue myself using the most simple, trusted and consistently effective strategy for these scenarios which, as any man knows, is to wheel out truckloads of compliments.

"What I meant was that you don't need all those lotions and potions to look great, sweetie. You're a natural beauty. Just recently you look better than ever!" I said as earnestly as I could manage. She softened a bit and grunted something inaudible.

"You even look like you've slimmed down a bit," I went on.

"Do you think so?" she squinted at me.

"Yeah, really."

"Hm. I think I did lose some weight, on the Ilha do Mel. It was the healthy living and eating," she reflected. "My *bunda* is still a bit generous though, I could do with losing some more. Do you remember, at the start of the trip, when I was a little bit big?"

"Uh-huh," I said, absent-mindedly.

"You thought I was big at the start of the trip?!" she suddenly shot at me.

Oh crap. "No, I mean, what? Was that a trick question? No, I didn't think you were big at the start of the trip. Of course I didn't!"

"*All* questions are trick, Joss. Haven't you learned that by now? You think I was big at the start of the trip." She went into a small huff again. I gave up.

I was already aware of the necessity to limit what we carried. Loading our bags into the van, the number of things we needed seemed insane. It would all have to get sorted when we joined the others. I almost yearned for the simpler life that beckoned us in the Patagonian pine forests, where we would find out for ourselves what was essential and otherwise.

On the way out of town, I filled the tank and two jerry cans with E25, the Brazilian gasoline and alcohol mix, and we continued on our way. The mountains gave way to estancias and wetlands dotted with cattle as we neared the border with Uruguay. Crossing the border at Chuí, the mood changed from the dust, chaos and life of the Brazilian side to the sombre and ordered Uruguayan half of town. We picked up food supplies in the cheaper Brazilian stores, completed border formalities and drove an hour or so beyond the frontier.

We spent our first night camping in the van at an old whale lookout on the long, desolate beach north of Punta del Diablo. The bed was warm and comfortable and, still full of energy from our sedentary day, we inaugurated it as was fitting for the moment, then re-inaugurated it. We read in silence afterwards by the light of our head torches. I was reading Charrière's *Banco*. Tina had renewed her involvement with Isabel Allende's *Cuentos de Eva Luna*, with the aim of improving her Spanish, now that we were back out of the Portuguese-speaking world.

In a short time, we were asleep. We slept to the sound of howling wind and crashing waves, Little Billie rocking gently with the wind as though at sea.

~~~~~

We arose early with the sound of rain drumming on the roof. Weary at the prospect of another full day's drive, we were nonetheless keen to get it done and dragged ourselves up and off. The others were arriving from Italy in two days. We had sent instructions for them to meet us in Tigre, the town just to the north of Buenos Aires, where the great delta of the Paraná River meets the River Plate. We drove for twelve hours through mixed farmland and Pampas. The rain stopped after six. We finally reached Carmelo, our objective, from where we would take the ferry in the morning.

"Uruguay is boring," Tina complained, stretching her arms up and arching her back.

I was inclined to agree but elected to give the place the benefit of the doubt. "That's just the long journey talking, there's still a lot of it we haven't seen."

Tina persisted. "But it's no Brazil. I *loved* Brazil. What if Patagonia is this boring?"

I knew how hard Tina had found it to leave Brazil. She had unfinished business there. I hoped that events would permit me the chance to fulfil the promise I had made to her that we would return there together one day.

"It won't be," I reassured her. "We'll be with all the others and there are loads of mountains and forests, it's beautiful. Anyway, you'll be happy to be somewhere boring if Brazil starts falling apart like everywhere else is at the moment. It's a crazy enough country at the best of times!"

Tina looked truculent. "Ugh! It's so stuuupid!" she sighed, resting her head on the dashboard.

"Yeah, you're not wrong," I concurred. "Unfortunately, we live in stupid times, which is why we have to get ourselves as far away from trouble as possible and sit things out. It seems a bit far-fetched, but it's only far-fetched until it actually happens." Tina did not move from the dashboard.

We found a small hotel in Carmelo and stayed the night there. Showered and fresh in the morning, we put Little Billie on a ferry and chugged through the verdant delta of the Paraná towards Tigre. The channels were the highways in this part of the world and it, like Kay's island, seemed unaffected so far by all the madness elsewhere in the world. A deep olive-skinned local sitting next to me was watching me observe the banks as we went, and seemed to read my thoughts.

"*Amigo*, in ten years none of these people will be here. Not the children going to school in the kayaks, nor the floating shops in the river boats, nor the water taxis, nothing. It is not obvious but the people are already leaving. Every year, the Río de la Plata is bringing higher and higher tides, with the higher sea. Every year, the Río Paraná is bringing more and more rain from Brazil – there is not enough forest left to drink it. The people of this delta are in the middle and, *blas!*" His dark eyes flashed beneath thick, black eyebrows as he made a crashing motion with the palms of his hands and his forearms, which were exceptionally hairy. He wore his shirt with the sleeves rolled up, like me. I nodded and looked back at the houses on stilts on the bank.

"Where are they going?" I asked.

"Most to Buenos Aires, where else?" he said, "But I will go to Patagonia, in one year or two. I will have a farm."

I raised my eyebrow. "Why to Patagonia?"

He smiled. "There is more chance to make a new life, there are not so many people there. And it is more safe from this kind of thing, I think." He pointed at the river.

I instinctively sized him up. This was the competition. I shouldn't think of it that way.

"*Bueno, amigo. Suerte.* I wish you luck," I replied. I felt a little on edge. Inevitably, we weren't the only ones that would make our way south, but I asked myself how many others had the same idea. Damn it, there were just too many people. Something had to happen, we'd stick with the plan and see where it took us.

The plan, I repeated to myself, and I thought of Robinson.

XI

Joe and the others arrived the next day, a day of brilliant blue skies and sunshine. I had told them to get the coastal train from the Retiro station in Buenos Aires up to the small station at Tigre. They arrived in the afternoon, stepping off the brightly coloured carriages, looking tanned, relaxed and still buzzing from their time in the Apennines. There were strong embraces all round, the strongest from Neil, who lifted both me and Tina off the ground at the same time, while growling affectionately.

Neil introduced us to Frederica, who I liked instantly. She was a touch shorter than his five feet ten, with wide, dark, intelligent eyes and chestnut hair, cut short. The hair gave her a slightly tomboyish look, set off by her jeans and t-shirt. She always wore the hint of a smile, which kept you guessing at what was amusing her and which made you want to smile too.

They propped their rucksacks against a table on the decking of the café by the station and we ordered coffees, sparkling waters and beers.

There was too much to catch up on. Joe got everything going. "This is a bit low-key. I was expecting there to be a big *fiesta* with loads of coke and scantily clad dancers and drummers to welcome us. This is South America, after all." He shimmied his broad shoulders in jest.

"Sorry to disappoint, Joe. That's happening later this evening," was the best I could manage in response.

Neil reached into his backpack and pulled out a dropper of the kind used for nasal drops. "Don't worry, this'll keep us going till then. I mix mine with saline and carry it in this. Gets past the scans and dogs every time." He put a drop in each nostril and sniffed. "Should be old enough to know better by now, but I'm not!" he whooped, and let out a belly laugh that nearly deafened everyone.

Joe looked intrigued and tried a drop himself. He chuckled and fist-bumped his brother, who put the dropper away again.

I hated cocaine and what it did to the majority of those involved with it, turning them into false people, aloof and aggressive. Neil was, so far, an exception. I couldn't help but smile at his audacity. "What about Italy, then?" I asked Joe.

"Oh, yeah. Don't know where to begin really. Freddie's place in the hills was amazing, we had the best time there. It was like stepping back in time two hundred years. Just imagine your ideal of Italian rural life and you're more or less there. Medieval castles and villages on hill tops, crickets buzzing in the countryside, poppies everywhere. Hot, sleepy afternoons with no one around. Good, *tasty*, proper food." Freddie looked delighted as she watched and listened to him speak of her home. "What else? Lots of eye candy for Ny," he nudged her a few times with his elbow as she protested her innocence, "and the two of us discovered that it's better if she sits on the back of the moped rather than me when we're going up the steep, windy hills they have around there," he chuckled again, holding up a grazed forearm, "and then," he carried on, "there was this. Just the local tipple, we loved it, drank barrels of it!" With a flourish, he pulled out a bottle of red wine which Neil uncorked gracefully and poured into our water glasses. We cheers-ed with the Italian "*Salute!*" It was light and refreshing – perfect for the hot weather.

In contrast to the rural idyll they had enjoyed in the mountains, they told us of the chaos at the airport in Rome. There had been fights over places on overbooked planes, huge queues, heavy security and offers of refunds on tickets, but they had eventually managed to get checked in, courtesy of some diplomacy at the counter on Freddie's part.

She spoke of the general situation in Italy. "People, they are either going back to the country or they are leaving. In Italy, the family is the most important. If they have family in Australia, in Argentina, in the United States, they are going there. If they have family in the countryside or in *Sicilia* or in Sardinia, then they are going there. Also, many foreigners are returning home, to Argentina and other places. It is like we are returning to older times. Those ones that are left in the cities are beginning to have a problem, everything is not working well. There are already things that they cannot buy, other than in the street."

"That's the problem in Britain," said Neil. "There's not the same strong family. How many people keep in contact with their cousins? How many people have even got normal families to go back to? Who's got the choice of going to the country? The countryside in England at the moment is full of farmers patrolling their fields at night with shotguns to stop people stealing their animals."

"And their vegetables. All the runner beans were taken from our allotment," interrupted Nyree in her soft Kiwi voice. "They weren't even ready to eat!"

Neil nodded. I could see from the wild glint in his eye that he had lost none of his edge. If anything, he looked sharper than ever. "It's every man for himself mate, seriously. I was speaking with my mate Sark, he lives in Newcastle, they've had *drone strikes* up there. You won't see it in the news, but a load of people saw it happen."

"There's no point even reading the news," Joe stated matter-of-factly.

We celebrated the fact that we'd all made it to where we were, finished the wine and beers and, in the late afternoon warmth, walked the short distance to the hostel and camp site where the Kombi was parked. Neil was the first to make the deduction.

"Mate, is that our wheels?" he blasted in my ear. He had the most booming voice I had ever known — more booming, even, than Robinson.

"We're motorised!" I nodded back at him and he roared with an unrestrained laugh.

"So much for hiding out in the country, we're going to stick out like boners! But I love it!" He tackled me to the ground and knuckled the top of my head, as he was inclined to do at times like this, a throwback to days of being an older and bigger brother to Joe. Tina took the keys from my pocket, as I struggled in vain, and opened up the van to give the others the short tour of our new home. Nyree, especially, was thrilled, and set about giving Little Billie some homely touches: a bear mascot from Italy on the dashboard, patterned headscarves of her own tied around the front head rests and a string of beads tied to the stub where the rear view mirror had once been. It was determined amongst the girls that she and Joe would be the ones to sleep in the van first, while the others of us would sleep in the two tents we had between us.

We cooked a big spaghetti Bolognese using the hostel kitchen and sat around the table after eating, discussing plans and evaluating our kit situation over more wine and beers. Neil approved of the medical kit I had put together.

"Good work mate, it probably just needs some anti-histamine tablets and cream, I react badly to bites sometimes. We can pick some up, Freddie speaks Spanish."

"¿Si?" I looked over at Freddie.

"It's quite similar to Italian, I think," she said modestly.

Neil went on, "I've brought a few inhalers for me as well. I hardly ever use them, but just in case."

I acknowledged with a nod. Neil had suffered from asthma as a child. "That sounds like everything, then. With the insects, I'm hoping we won't have too many down that far south, it'll be too cold for them. That was another of the things counting in favour of going there. We might suffer a bit of cold, but we're less likely to pick up illnesses in a place like that than in somewhere like the jungle. Did you bring warm stuff to wear?"

"Yeah, and fire-lighting tools and a few other things," replied Neil, pulling out a utility belt. In conventional times, he was a carpenter and builder. He had spent his early adulthood making his way around the world doing whatever work he could find, including some years as a safari guide in Botswana. "I didn't pick up many tools because of the baggage allowance, but we'll get axes and saws and chisels anywhere."

Joe had acquired all of the electronic equipment requested, the global positioning system, the satellite internet hub, the solar chargers and some phones that we could use to navigate the web. I was startled at how he had achieved this so effortlessly with everything else that had been happening.

"What do we owe you, chief?" I asked.

Joe locked his fingers across his stomach and leaned back in his chair. "Don't worry about it," he said. "Our money's going to be worth nothing soon. I moved a lot of mine into Chinese bonds and currency just before all the markets crashed and that saved me from losing quite a bit. It's irrelevant longer term though. Weapons, tools, animals and food. These are going to be the new currencies."

I admired Joe's ability to play the system. "Alright Confucius, as long as we're quits for now. I was lucky, I had big shorts on some stocks just before the crash so I made a lot on those."

"I've moved all my savings to my Kiwi account," Nyree piped up. "So long as China's alright, so's NZ." She pronounced this *In Zid*. "Everything it produces: wood, milk, fruit, everything goes there."

Neil looked around, slightly bemused by all the talk of money. "I haven't got any money, so I'm not worried about losing any!" he laughed, and we toasted that.

"Why's this place called Tigre?" asked Joe.

I knew the answer from the conversation I had continued with the local on the ferry. "There's a wild cat that lives in the delta called a *Jaguarundi*. It looks a bit like a small tiger, hence the name *Tigre*. They only live right up in the upper reaches now, beyond the grasp of people and hunters."

Joe looked impressed. "Nature's way. When people are giving you trouble, retreat to where they can't reach you. It's what we're all doing here, pretty much. The only problem is when there's nowhere left to retreat to, and then there's no choice but to... crush your enemies!"

He raised his glass of wine. "Small tigers," he said, and we drank to small tigers.

XII

For the next few days we rested in Tigre and made final preparations for our journey south, taking advantage of the amenities on offer nearby in the capital. We bought maps, books on Patagonian flora and fauna and a Kombi maintenance manual in Portuguese, which Neil pored over for hours. Joe picked up a pile of assorted preserved delicacies that we may not find in smaller towns, including artichokes, sun-dried tomatoes in oil, olive tapenades, anchovies and capers, saying that we needed them for trace nutrients. Then there was the outdoor kit that we were still lacking: down sleeping bags, bivouac bags, rubber boots, axes, slingshots, hunting knives, fishing rods and tackle. Neil picked up the woodworking tools he was missing. Nyree and Tina worked on making Little Billie more homely than ever and turned the inside into something resembling a Bedouin tent, with a dividing curtain between front and back for the night time, pull curtains on the back windows, cushions and handmade pillow cases and bedding covers for the bed and bunks, everything in bright colours and patterns.

If in doubt, take it all out. We loaded and unloaded

the Kombi dozens of times in different configurations and performed test runs on both asphalt and gravel roads, running the engine on both gasoline and alcohol. There was always so much to do. Neil, a good mechanic from his time in Africa, serviced and tweaked the vehicle to his satisfaction as I watched and learned that there is always more that can be done on an engine. Freddie volunteered as head chef and turned out beautiful Italian food each afternoon, assisted by the Italian delicatessens that she had discovered on her trips into Buenos Aires. Joe became absorbed in books on South American history and would offer us interesting morsels from his reading from time to time. Nyree talked on her phone a lot in the mornings. Tina liked to keep a detailed diary of everything that happened and could often be found writing, and she enjoyed learning Freddie's culinary secrets.

I spent time along with Joe, examining maps, satellite images and climate charts for potential locations for us to base ourselves down south. It was all provisional of course, the plan was to find a cabin, maybe even a cave, in the mountains below the treeline, in which to live. What could be achieved through research was limited.

I was reassured by the thought that technology was still no match for local knowledge. There would always remain pockets of people living on local knowledge no matter what happened to our civilization. Nomadic reindeer herders in the Siberian wilderness, subsistence farming communities in Bhutan, hunter-gatherer tribes in the forests of New Guinea, sea gypsies in the archipelagos of Oceania. These peoples existed, and their ways of life, while so distant from us as to appear almost fictional, had the perhaps decisive advantage of the incredible resilience that comes from a lack of dependence on the outside world.

Our van unloaded once more, I was suddenly struck

by a vision of the chasm that we had to cross to achieve a return to an independent way of life. This abyss was embodied by our piles of tinned food, electronics, clothes, tools and our vehicle. A sense of helplessness passed over me momentarily. How weak we were that, even stripped down to the bare bones, we felt we could not survive without these things. How pathetically dependent we were on the services offered by the city. How tied we still were to the *programme*.

Neil's thundering voice knocked me out of my reverie. After a ceremonious shave, which had lasted an hour, in the wing mirror of the Kombi, with a basin of boiling water and a beautiful straight razor with leaves of olive wood that he had brought with him, he'd been working on the van all morning. "Hey, goof, chuck me that screwdriver by your foot would you? This back door handle's loose."

I threw him the screwdriver. "Here you go. How's Li'l Billie altogether?" The van's name was popular with everyone and had stuck.

"Good mate, she's ready to go. I love these Flex engines, they're awesome. I don't understand why we don't have them everywhere. You can make your own alcohol. Forget petrol."

"It's all switching to electric rather than alcohol, in most places," I commented.

Neil snorted. "Where are you going to plug in an electric when you're out in the sticks? You're better off with a donkey and cart. Electric wouldn't be any use where we're going."

"It's a question of priorities," said Joe enigmatically. He had been sitting in a deck chair reading for several hours. "Not everyone's a hillbilly who spends their time driving around on farms. Electric is the best technology for most people in most countries because most people live in cities. If we all drove alcohol cars, there'd be no forests left or food to eat because we'd grow nothing but biofuel crops."

Neil looked at him with disdain. "I don't know what your priorities are, lard arse. Why don't you get up and do something? And get Ny to help out as well, she just yaks on the phone all day, it must be costing a mental amount."

We could hear Nyree talking on her phone in the background between tracks from the Kombi's sound system, which Neil worked to.

Joe frowned as he carried on reading. "This *is* work, meathead. Just because I'm not dressed in some cack-stained overalls and hitting something with a wrench, it doesn't mean I'm not *doing* anything. Knowledge is power. Ny's working, too."

Neil wore an expression of utter bemusement. "*Working?*" he almost spat, "Doing *what?*"

Joe didn't look up from his book. "She's doing her Reiki thing, she's started doing it for dogs."

Neil put down the screwdriver. "Please tell me you're making this up. *Reiki* for *dogs*, and she's doing it over the *phone?!*"

Nyree appeared as though summoned, gliding across the grass separating where our camp was from the communal area. She wore a flowing dress and light cardigan and gave us all a smile before pulling up a deck chair alongside Joe.

"Tell these guys about the remote thing you've got

going, Ny," he said to her.

She looked at both of us, hesitating. "Oh, yeah, I was starting to do it before we came away to, like, save all the travelling around to clients and stuff. But, when I advertised it on the web site, I got calls from people I'd never treated before wanting the remote service too. That one I was on the phone to just now was from Paris!"

Neil looked pained. "A dog?"

"Yeah, by video call," Nyree responded calmly. "He's a real terrorist of a little thing, but he's responding well to the sessions. They're the only time of the week that he totally behaves."

"And what do you charge for that?" enquired Neil.

"A hundred and fifty euros that session," Nyree replied as though this was completely normal, "I've brought it down a bit, but it's still not bad."

Neil glanced to me for support but, for me, seeing his exasperation was my entertainment. I just laughed and shrugged, "Why not?"

Neil liked dogs and had something of a natural affinity with them. He had been known back in England, on many occasions, to play-wrestle with people's pet dogs on pavements in crowded streets and in parks. When he spotted a dog that looked game for a wrestle, he would rush over to it without warning and drop to his knees barking and howling, taking its front legs in his hands and starting the contest. This would usually leave a bemused and unacknowledged owner looking on while Neil rolled around on the ground with their dog. Nobody knew how he had developed this behaviour, but he did not seem to consider it out of the ordinary, and it was brilliant to watch. He got up, leaving the back door handle of the

Kombi on the ground and went and held out a fist for a knuckle high-five with Nyree. She bumped her fist against his.

"I give up. Gotta hand it to you, Ny, that's genius," he growled and chuckled to himself, shaking his head. "Reiki for dogs over the phone! The world is an even madder place than I thought. Who wants a beer? Freddie and Tina will be back from town soon." He walked off to the fridge to get us all beers.

~~~~~

We decided over another of Freddie's superb late lunches that we would depart the next day. There was an impalpable tension growing over Buenos Aires where, as in other places, the stock markets and currency were in trouble. On the crowded *Calle Florida*, where shady illegal money changers plied their trade from doorways, people had been urgently buying US dollars and Tina and I had done a good trade, returning to a changer that we knew from our previous stay in the city and selling some of our dollars at far above the official exchange rate. "Each time we pick ourselves up, we are beaten to our knees again," he had told me.

We got the maps out on the table after lunch and all settled on the stubby finger of Argentine territory, north-west of Esquel and protruding into Chile, as the place we would travel to first. It was far from any roads and had heavy forests, abundant water, and deep, sheltered mountain valleys. If it was not right, there were alternatives further south, but in August, the depths of Patagonian Winter, the further down we went, the harsher the elements would be.

That night, in our tent, I fell asleep with Tina in my arms. In a dream, I came into being high up in a pink sky, above layers of smooth, flat clouds that also reflected pink in the light. Snowy mountaintops protruded through the platforms of cloud, and below me in all directions were skeins of geese flying in V-formation making their way towards the sunset. I swooped down and joined one of them. We flew like this for a long time. There was the constant honking of calls from the other geese, and we would frequently change positions in the formation. Sometimes one of the birds in front of me or to the side would drop out of the skein and slowly fall beneath the clouds. Other birds would join us from above. We carried on flying towards the setting sun, racing to catch it.

XIII

We awoke with the light of another brilliantly fine day coming through the green fabric of the tent. It was already hot inside. I unzipped the inner and outer doors to allow the fresh air in and took a look outside. The others were up and Joe was frying eggs and bacon, sending a mouth-watering aroma over to where we were. When I retreated back inside to lie down, Tina was performing the morning ritual of arranging her afro, a process of a thousand imperceptibly small adjustments using the fingertips of both hands.

"Today's the day my louve! Are you looking forward to it? You look crumpled!" she observed.

The question caused memories of Patagonia to spring into my mind. I hiked through purple heather amid mountains, fierce winds whipping over lakes beneath pristine skies, causing rainbows to dance across their surfaces. Cannons boomed in the night as icebergs calved from glaciers. I navigated the channels of the fjords through fog, glimpsing brilliant blue ice formations spilling into silent inlets. I saw, in black and white photos, the faces of the Kawésqar people that once lived their whole lives on the frigid ocean in wooden canoes, with open fires and children on board and the women covering their bodies in seal fat to dive for oysters.

"Yeah. And you?" I croaked, bleary-eyed.

"What's not to look forward to? Road trip!" she chirped. It was her turn to be the bright one this morning. "Come on, Crumps."

We put on flipflops and walked over the grass to the camp site kitchen where everyone else was sitting around the table.

"Mushrooms with your bacon and eggs?" asked Joe. "Do it," I said, and Tina nodded.

Neil, already mopping up egg yolks with a piece of bread, piped up. "Before we head, has anyone looked at the news to check that everything's not hunky dory again? Maybe we can just go surfing."

"I did last night," Nyree spoke. "The UK's still bad. People've brought down some motorway bridges in the North somewhere. The government had to admit to the drone strikes and since then they're saying that some soldiers are going AWOL, refusing to serve."

"Vish," said Neil through a mouthful of bread. Frederica caught his eye. He gulped his bread down and laid his arms across her shoulders, looking guilty. "Err, I mean, that's terrible," he corrected himself, rolling his eyes theatrically as he did so.

"You're a terrible person!" she half-chastised him.

"Thanks, sweetheart," he squeezed her as she screwed up her face, attempting to avoid the egg yolk on his chin.

He looked like he'd enjoy being back home and part of the action. "Looks like it's all go then. Who's driving?"

"You can Steelie, she's your baby now," I said to Neil as Joe lay down my plate on the table. "Thanks, Mum," I thanked him. The first mouthful of hot bacon and soft egg yolk immediately improved my outlook. Then, looking back at Neil, "I bagsy a seat up front though. I'll navigate."

"I'll do tunes!" Tina snuck in quickly.

After our breakfast, we washed up, had brief, cold showers, stowed away our tents and sleeping bags, settled with the camp site and jumped into the Billie wagon. Neil sat in the driver's seat, Tina was in the middle and I was by the right window. Joe, Freddie and Nyree had a lot of room to lie down and move around in the back. There was an electricity in the air and a sense of the momentousness of the present. Nobody wanted to kill it, but it felt like it should be marked. We wound down the windows. Neil put on his wrap-around shades and started the engine, making the bear mascot on the dashboard shake. "Speech, Joe, Bru!" he roared above the judder of the motor.

Joe was good at times like this and, moreover, enjoyed them. He smiled and repositioned himself with a meaty elbow leaning on the backrest of the front seat. He thought for a few moments and visibly focused before starting.

"The world in our time is not harmonious – things are broken. Do we accept it or do we change it? Acquiesce with a deranged world and you yourself become deranged. Remaking the world is for gods, though, and we are buttmen."

He snickered at his own double-entendre. Substituting "butt" for "but" was something he'd been unable to resist doing ever since school. He continued with his oratory:

"So, what choices remain? You cannot catch the wind, but let it carry you and you will catch your prey. While our direction changes, our compass points true. By choice we change ourselves, change I *our* worlds. We drop a gauntlet before the wind of destiny and raise our Billie-sail. We men embrace what lies before us, our women embrace what stands before them. It's not where we *are* that matters, but where *we* are. ROOOAAAARRRR!"

"Very good! *Bravo!*" cheered Freddie. We all clapped and banged our fists on the seats and dashboard. Ha, I now knew why he had the compass on his arm.

"I'm assuming the butt-men thing was intended as an erudite counterpoint to Thoreau's 'We are a race of tit-men', Joe?" I joked, pleased with my reference.

"That's right!" answered Joe, accepting the credit and soaking up the appreciation of his speech. He took a small, seated bow in the back of the van.

"Can you put me down as a tit-man? I'm more aligned with Thoreau," said Neil.

Tina hit us with Steppenwolf's *Born to be Wild* on the sound system, a track that she mocked me for liking but secretly enjoyed herself, and with a lurch and a roar from Little Billie, we were at last on the road.

XIV

We took the road out towards Santa Rosa, through the vastness of the Pampa, aiming after that for Neuquén and then Bariloche. There, we would join the partly paved roads that paralleled the dendritic spine of mountains delimiting the western edge of Argentine Patagonia and the frontier with Chile. The camp sites in the small towns on the road south were mostly closed for the winter so we would pull up off the road in the evenings, pitch tents and practice preparing meals from our stores, testing our cooking equipment, taking note of refinements that needed to be made and extra supplies that needed to be picked up. The only annoyance was the omnipresent semi-feral dogs. They came during the night, even when we were miles from anywhere, rooting around for scraps of food, so we learned to keep our camp very clean.

We all shared in the driving, cooking, washing up and cleaning. Little Billie was cleaned and aired at the end of each day's driving, to stave off the ripeness that came from having six bodies inside. After four days, when we reached the quiet town of Neuquén, we stopped for two nights in a guesthouse. We took showers and laundered our clothes, and picked up extra herbs and spices, bottles of hot pepper sauce, aluminium foil, extra plastic bags and boxes – all the small things we had overlooked while in Tigre. I ran and exercised with Neil and Joe in the mornings, doing bicep curls with rucksacks, pull-ups on beams and shuttle runs holding boxes over our heads to counter the long hours spent travelling. In the evenings we ate at a local *parrilla* grill and gorged on the outstanding *bife de chorizo* steaks, which we ordered *jugoso*, or literally, "juicy". There was home-made gnocchi and *morcilla* blood sausages, of which Joe would eat three in a sitting. Afterwards, there was local cheese with stringy *alcayota* marrow jam. Everything was good.

~~~~~

This was a land of big, empty skies and wide horizons. From Neuquén, we were back on the road. We left on another bright morning, Tina at the wheel with the two other girls up front, talking. Joe was laid out snoozing on one of the back bunks, myself and Neil sat on the other. I watched the landscape go by from the back window for maybe an hour. It changed little, and was mostly dry and brown. I was somewhat restless, unable to allow my mind to drift off as would normally happen at these times. Looking over at Neil, he was evidently bored, eavesdropping the girls' conversation for titbits. After some time, Joe's phone rang in his pocket. Neil, with lightning reflexes, grabbed it before his brother had time to come around and held it up, taunting him.

"Who is it?!" he cooed, pretending to read from the screen. "Wait! Ny? Ny? Do you know who this is... *'Text-Flirt Nympho Ex #2'?!*" He leaned forward and rested his chin on the back of the front seat expectantly, holding the phone at arm's length.

Joe sat up. "Juuuuuvey," he groaned. "Just answer it,

nobbo, before it stops ringing."

Tina turned down the volume of the music on the stereo. "It's Red!" announced Neil and answered it. "Redface!" he shouted above the drone of the engine, "What's up you big, fat chopper?"

I watched Neil as he spoke to Red. He listened for a long time, nodding, then eventually spoke. "Painful, mate, fucking jobsworths. You've got twelve hours did you say? Right, yeah, listen, I'll speak with the others here. Don't worry, we'll call you back in a bit."

"Jeeeeezus," he puffed as he ended the call. "Get this, Red's in Canada with Jen. They won't let her into the country, some horseshit about renewing her status while they were living abroad. They've given her twelve hours to get on a plane out of there. He's going with her, obviously. They're thinking of coming down here."

It seemed clear what we had to do. We'd wait for them while they made their way down to us. We needed everyone to agree, though, and for this we'd stop so we could have a proper discussion. While feeling for Red and Jen, and their difficult situation, I was glad that this twist of fate would mean them joining us. They were good people, a blast to have around and, on top of that, we'd be stronger with them. Red had grown up in rural Ontario and had spent much of his youth in the wilderness of lakes and forests in that state and in neighbouring Quebec. He was a good outdoorsman, despite having traded his woods and rivers for the sprawling megalopolis of Seoul. He had an irrepressible optimism complemented by a natural irreverence. If he had a serious side at all, which I doubted, it was very rarely glimpsed.

Jen was a quiet girl but as tough as leather. If you looked closely, her rosy cheeks and surprisingly strong legs betrayed some clues as to her past. She disliked large groups of people. She would speak for hours alone with Red in a soft voice, but would usually go silent if there were other people around, preferring to absorb what was going on around her. It was because she was conscious of her imperfect English, Red told us. On the occasions I had spoken at length with her, I had discovered an energising vitality and sense of humour that often lay hidden beneath her calm, inscrutable exterior. When this impassiveness gave way to bursts of giggles, as it often did, it was a joy to behold. She would also bring with her a background of an early life spent on the Mongolian steppe, priceless knowledge where we were going.

"Pull over when you get a chance, T!" I called up to Tina, "Emergency high council!"

"Aye, skip!" she called back cheerfully and brought Little Billie to a stop on a stony patch of level ground alongside the road a short way further up. Freddie broke out the big flask of hot chocolate she had prepared that morning and we jumped out of the van to stretch our legs, sitting in a circle on the dry, brown grass alongside the clearing.

Our custom of holding high councils, as we called them, to make important decisions or interventions, had begun years before when there had been a fall-out between Red and Joe's old girlfriend Fiona, she of the hair-straighteners. It was innocuous enough at first. It was before Red moved to Korea, and he was living in London and working in a Canadian pub in Covent Garden. We had all gone there for a long weekend to see him. We were outside in the garden of the pub where he worked, eating and enjoying the odd beer on the house. Red was swinging a foot absent-mindedly under the table, his toe tapping what he thought was one of the wooden struts beneath it. It turned out, however, that this was Fiona's leg. After enduring it for a short while, she crossly pointed out to him that he was kicking her shin. Being Red, to try and alleviate the situation he tapped her leg a couple of times with his toe a few minutes later, hoping she'd lighten up. This backfired spectacularly, causing her a complete sense of humour meltdown and to call him an "ignorant cretin", and from there, escalating into what became known as "Toegate". From that day forward, Fiona refused to speak to Red ever again, despite his profuse apologies. It got so absurd that we devised the concept of a high council to attempt to address the issue. We held the inaugural council at Joe's house, with Red present, to try to persuade Fiona to relax her stance. She never really did, and it was not long later that she left Joe, causing him all kinds of problems of the heart and sending him into his misogynistic lost period. The whole thing had left a bad taste, and even now it felt slightly sordid to recall it, although it made a mildly amusing tale. Nobody missed her and her dramas much. It's best to get rid of the negative influences in your life, for that's what she was. However, the councils that she had inadvertently initiated stayed with us.

At our high council by the roadside with hot chocolate, there was unanimous agreement that Red and Jen should team up with us, even from Freddie, who had never met either of them. "They seem nice from what you say," she sang in her pleasant voice. My early fears that Freddie wouldn't stand up to the hardships of the trip were proving completely groundless, and I was irked at myself for having doubted her. She was treating everything as a great adventure, putting her heart into it and loving every minute, helped by Neil who, in his rough-edged way, adored her. Of course, having Red and Jen in the van would mean more of a squeeze, as well as buying extra supplies and an extra tent, but no-one was bothered by this. Joe phoned Red back on the spot. He and Jen would make their way to Buenos Aires or Santiago in Chile and from there on to Bariloche, where we would wait and expect them.

XV

Driving in the afternoon, following the high council, the dry plains finally began to give way to hills and rivers on the way to Bariloche, and the country became fresher and greener. Rounding the southern shore of the giant lake, Nahuel Huapi, on the approach to the city, we joined the end of a long, stationary line of traffic. Nyree, who had switched with Tina and was now driving, pulled up the hand brake and turned off the engine. We could see the queue stretching over a rise bordering the lakeshore ahead of us. Beyond the lake and its islands, the black and white, snow-covered peaks of the Andes defined the horizon. We were still a few miles out of town and could not work out where all the people had come from.

Half an hour later we had advanced the few hundred yards to the top of the rise, mostly, it seemed, thanks to vehicles doing U-turns ahead of us. It was now dusk and, rubbing the condensation from the windows, we saw the line of cars, trucks and vans stretching as far as we could see in front and behind us, their red and white lights beginning to form a sparkling filament following the lakeside. Joe was enlightening us with historical tales he had read of the Machete River, one of those that flowed into the lake.

I got up and opened the back door. An icy gasp of air rushed into the van. "I'm going to go and see what's happening."

"Want some company?" offered Tina.

"It's alright, babe, stay here. It's cold."

I pulled on my hooded, dark grey, woollen jumper and olive-grey canvas jacket and got out, closing the door behind me. Following the line of vehicles ahead of us, I walked past opportunistic carts on the roadside that were selling corn-cobs, popcorn and carbonated drinks to where a circle of men, mostly truck drivers I guessed from their demeanour, were conversing. I hoped that the presence of a gringo would not discourage them from talking and that the unrefined appearance I had cultivated since coming away would count for me. My dark hair, which I had left to grow since well before leaving my work, was now long, with wave-like curls. My beard, too, was becoming strong and had streaks of copper and gold burned into it, at the sides of the moustache and on the tuft beneath my lower lip, from the intense Brazilian sunshine we had seen. "Like a tiger", I liked to kid to Tina.

The group looked at me suspiciously as I got close but eased as I drew a packet of cigarettes from the inside pocket of my jacket. I barely ever smoked but kept a box in my pocket when in foreign lands, for just such times as these.

"¿Che, tenés fuego?" I asked the least formidable-looking smoker among the collection, a chubby type with a smiling face and eyes that almost looked closed above his round cheeks. He held up a lighter. I puffed, resisting the tremendous urge to cough as I inhaled the bitter smoke, and offered around the open box, a couple of men taking cigarettes.

"Where are you from?" the one with the lighter asked me. "Not from around here!" he stated.

"Holland," I lied, choosing the nationality most likely to elicit a warm reaction that I could think of.

"Ah, alright Clogs," he chuckled, and turned his attention back to the circle. I stepped back half a foot from the edge and tuned my ears into the discussion to see if I could pick up on anything.

"... they've been wanting to do it since all the way back to the time of *Las Malvinas*, they've just been waiting for their chance," continued an old, thick-set, clean-shaven man in a parka who had been speaking when I arrived. "Everyone's got so many problems in their own yard at the moment that nobody will do anything about it. They'll take our mountains down here in the South for the glaciers and fresh water, then they'll take the rest of the *Tierra del Fuego*, for control of the Southern Ocean and the Antarctic Peninsula, and the fishing. Then they'll take our northern grain belt. They won't bother with anything else. We'll end up as a little patch of desert and Pampa on the Atlantic coast, with next to nothing."

"Like Uruguay!" laughed the man who had given me a light.

"It's happening all over," chimed in a small, wiry individual drinking *maté* through a metal straw from a vessel fashioned from a large, hollow seed. "The Americans have got a dirty fight on their hands against the narco-states. China's growing and patiently subsuming all that lies around it, while gently squeezing the resources out of everywhere else, even Argentina. The Russians are all over the Arctic Ocean while their country's on fire. They've even got their flag on the sea bed at the North Pole! One small move from anyone and it's World War Three."

A bearded, haggard man with his hands in his pockets and wearing a baseball cap spoke. "I don't give a shit about any of that. If that happens, we're all finished anyway. What I care about is getting to Chile. I had to be there three days ago and I've got a cargo of meat that's going to go off. My boss is having fits. I'm not going to get paid. They're not going to open this damned border. What are we supposed to do? What a terrible, wretched mess."

I felt myself flush hot as it dawned on me that the border with Chile had been closed. I hoped that Red and Jen hadn't gone that way. My mind raced. I was glad of the lack of daylight to hide my shock. "What about further south?" I ventured.

"You're going south? Don't bother," spoke the man with the *maté*, which he had topped up with hot water from a flask in his backpack. "They're only letting military, residents, workers and essential supplies pass through that way. You need to get a special permit. They've closed the whole border with Chile, they're preparing as though there's going to be an invasion. They've already called up the reserves. Conscription will start soon, you'll see. It'll be a winter war, like the *Malvinas*. You can go back home and watch it all on TV with a spliff. I'll give you a wave from my trench." This drew muted laughter from the gathering. "What the devil are you doing in this godforsaken place anyway?"

I reeled mentally at this unhappy news and avoided his question, instead rambling ill-advisedly about tactics in an attempt to change the subject. "Chile? You need to hit them first. Their weakness is their geography. It's impossible to defend a border that long and they can't be more than a few dozen kilometres wide in some places." Long hours spent examining maps of Patagonia had given me some knowledge of the geography of the region. "Strike at their narrowest points and cut off the parts from each other." I saw a few nods in the diffuse light that came from the headlights of the nearby vehicles.

"*Bien visto.* Good thinking, *Bonaparte,*" jibed the old man in the parka. "Now go to Buenos Aires and tell that to our shit-for-brains, drunken generals." A few men looked down at the floor. "I was in *Las Malvinas*, fighting the British. We had a lot of chances to win. Our problem now is the *pelotudos* at the top, just as it was then," he spat, using the Argentine insult that translates roughly as "wanker". He fixed me with a steely eye.

I nodded in deference to this veteran, thanking my prescience in not revealing my nationality. I judged that a retreat would be wise at this juncture. I had the information I needed. I drew deeply on my cigarette while I thought desperately of something to say. "You might have the biggest *pelotudos*, but you've got the biggest *pelotas* as well. I think you'll win," I joked, lying. The biggest balls. Perhaps my first improvised joke in Spanish. The veteran was unamused, but the others laughed, to my relief. "*Caballeros*, it has been a pleasure. Whatever comes to pass, I wish you all luck." I raised my hand and turned to walk back to the Kombi.

"*¡Igualmente, Bonaparte!*" came the faint reply from the gathering, amid more laughs.

Flicking the remains of my cigarette into the dirt, I opened the back door of the van and noticed for the first time that the handle was now secure and working properly. Neil must have fixed it up at some point. Inside, the others had put up the middle section of the bed, turning the back of the van into a comfortable den. They were playing Snatch, the word game that was currently our favourite way of passing long hours with nothing to do. I climbed up onto the bed using the back step and closed the door quickly to keep in the warmth, finding a spot in the corner and sitting cross-legged. As I took off my jacket, I was heartened to see that Kay's drop-top had been raised and was getting some use. Little Billie felt spacious and homely. I was experiencing a growing feeling of guilt at what I was going to have to tell everyone and decided to sit quietly and watch the game for a while.

It was a matter of seconds before my peace was rudely interrupted. "Joss, this is the worst holiday ever. *E-ver.* Where have you brought us?" Tina half-joked, looking at me with a smirk.

"Yeah, you *nob*," Neil emphasised comically without raising his head from the game.

These salvoes caught me completely off guard. Joe stopped studying the counters laid out in front of him and stared at me. "What passes, compadre? You're looking a bit serious," he murmured.

Hearing this, Neil, Freddie and Nyree looked over at me as well. There was no escape. I girded myself mentally for the coming discussion.

Sheepishly, I began to explain what I had learned on my excursion. "Guys. Girls. We've just encountered an obstacle."

XVI

"Bogus. Ten seconds into round one and we've just been punched in the face and knocked down," surmised Joe once I had brought everyone up to date with the conversation with the truck drivers. "We'd better phone Red straight away to check he hasn't gone to Chile, or he'll be stuck." He tapped at his phone.

The consensus was to sleep on the news and take up the discussion on what to do in the morning. Nobody seemed particularly concerned, just weary from waiting in the van. I was angry with myself for having focused all my attention on what had been happening in every part of the world other than the part where we were going, ignorantly assuming that the remoteness of Patagonia exempted it from the petty politics that pervaded in the more populated regions of the globe. If there was no sanctuary there, at the end of the Earth, where then? There had been no back-up plan. I was an amateur. It was embarrassing.

Joe found out that Red and Jen, fortuitously, were *en route* to Buenos Aires, via a number of countries. The game of Snatch was concluded in Tina's favour. She was a genius at it. The line of traffic did not move. We all slept in the Kombi.

~~~~~

We were awoken at dawn by the rumble of truck engines. The line moved a kilometre or so and then stopped again. We pulled over on a patch of waste ground, opened the doors to the crisp morning air and, shivering, got things out for breakfast. Ahead of us, up the road, I saw the bearded truck driver from the previous night barbequing some of the meat from his consignment, surrounded by a few of the others. Neil, macho as ever, disappeared to answer the call of nature carrying his wash bag and wearing only a t-shirt, flipflops and a sarong-like *kikoy*. He used the *kikoy* as a towel, a garment and to sleep in, a habit he had liked and had kept with him from his time in Botswana. His morning routines were always elaborate, another echo from his days in Africa, and particularly so on the days he chose to shave with his straight razor, a much-cherished object.

I wanted to wait until everyone was present to make an apology for this wild goose chase I had led them on, so decided to wait until Neil came back before calling them together. "I'm sorry, T," I whispered in her ear, my breath rising visibly in the chill air as I did so, "this was a bad place to come."

"Can we go back to Brazil now then?" she joked and prodded me in the ribs. I managed a weak smile but felt like I was carrying a wet bag of cement in my rib cage. I crouched and lit two camping stoves on the ground, the warm gas fumes causing me some dizziness, and began to make porridge on one and boil water for coffee on the other. I made the porridge with water and powdered milk, judging the quantities by eye, and loosened the lids of jars of jam and honey to accompany it. Joe stamped his boots and blew on his hands against the cold. Freddie went back into the van to get more warm clothes, swaddling herself in so many layers she was barely visible.

Neil returned after some time, joining the rest of us standing around the stoves drinking coffee and waiting for the porridge to cook. I had what I was going to say ready in my head and had butterflies in my stomach. I knew in my heart, which was racing involuntarily, that I had cocked things up. The others were just being kind to me. I cleared my throat to talk but Joe got in too quickly before me, calling over at Neil, "You were gone a long time. You weren't banging one out, were you?"

"Banging one out," repeated Frederica from behind her two scarves, and giggled. "Phrasal verb."

She lowered the scarves with the fingers of her right hand and took a sip of coffee from her metal mug. I had not noticed until now that she was left-handed.

There was no reply from Neil.

"You have an interview with the mafia this morning?" Joe asked him, making fun of his hair, which he had slicked back. Freddie giggled again.

"No, mate. I think I have a problem," announced Neil.

Tina frowned. "I think you have a lot of problems. Which one do you want to tell us about?"

"Erm. It's a bit embarrassing," smiled Neil, acting shy, building up to something.

"We know you've got a small willy, you've shown it to us enough times before," joked Tina. Freddie giggled again, the sound muffled through wool.

With this, Neil pulled open his *kikoy*, holding out the corners like wings. He had neatly painted his scrotum and male member with the mercurochrome from the medical kit so that they stood out in bright vermilion against his pale skin, as proud and prominent as a mandrill's backside. The brilliant display of colour somehow made the exhibition less indecent. There were screams from the girls that descended into side-splitting laughter, drawing looks from the people scattered up and down the roadside. Nyree was laughing so hard she was doubled up and had dropped her coffee. Joe raised his eyebrows.

"You need to go to the clinic," he said, deadpan, at which Nyree fell over, unable to breathe.

"I just woke up this morning and it was like this," said Neil. "I was thinking that maybe I've turned into the alpha male of our group, or something, and this is what happens. Tina, Ny, you're mine now too, like Freddie. Sorry Joss, Joe, that's just how it is. You're going to have to leave."

Nyree was hitting the ground with her foot, silently crying with laughter. When the urge to breathe became too strong, she drew an extended gasp and coiled up again, half-laughing, half-crying with a wailing noise, making even Neil chuckle.

"Trick I learned in Africa," he leaned over and winked at me. "Thought of it back when I saw the mercurochrome in your med kit. Remember, mate, the *mzungu* gets unhappy when his *programme* goes wrong. Don't worry about all this, it'll work out alright."

We hadn't decided anything, didn't know where we were going, but we were back on track, you could feel it, and knew it from the laughing. I bumped fists with Neil and trashed the speech I had prepared in my head. He had put us right. Words, I realised, aren't always necessary.

XVII

After breakfast, we piled into the Kombi and Neil fired up the motor. He berated the girls for allowing the fuel tank to run down to almost empty, and we got out while he retrieved one of our jerry cans from the back to top it up.

"You can't blame them. They're not like us," said Joe, standing by Neil as he funnelled the fuel into the tank. "It's a machine. Women have no concept of fuel or the necessity of keeping it topped up until it runs out. It's like blokes, when you move into a new house and it turns out that you need to paint the walls a different colour. You have no idea until your chick starts ear-bashing you about it."

We all jumped back in and Neil swung us around in a U-turn and accelerated away. When he drove, he would often steer using only one finger, the little finger of his left hand, on the bottom of the wheel, keeping the right hand free for gear changes. Sitting alongside Tina in the back, I could see that she had noticed this, and that it made her a little nervous, though she said nothing. She would brake with her bum cheeks from time to time, pre-empting Neil's own braking. At these times, I would clench my own buttocks and sit straight up, imitating her, to amuse myself. For this, I would receive jabs in the ribs from Tina. It was thus that we began to retrace our tracks along the long road we had followed from Santa Rosa. We had told Red and Jen to meet us there but had not planned any further than that. With two fresh brains and two new sets of ideas and perspectives we would all decide what to do together.

Two days later, in the early evening, we met them at the bus terminal of Santa Rosa. Catching sight of us, Red gave us his customary salute of "Howareya!" and gave us all bear hugs. Jen introduced herself to Frederica first and then emulated Red, giving us bear hugs, too. She was strong for a girl so slight and could lift Joe right off the ground. Both of them looked to be in rude health despite their long and tortuous journey. When they'd left their bags in the Kombi we went straight to the local grill to celebrate and catch up.

"Can you *believe*, man," stressed Red through a mouthful of the gigantic steak he had ordered, "that after four years of being married, we're still required to go back, both of us, in person, *every year*, to fill out a set of shitty forms and pay *eighteen hundred* dollars, not including the cost of the flights? In the age of the internet? They make you start the whole process from scratch every year. Goddam' it, it makes me angry just thinking about it. It's beyond reach."

Everyone nodded and shook their heads. It infuriated me to hear of such gratuitous bureaucracy. "Mate, that's *unbelievably* anally retentive. It's a pile of fuming BS wrapped in more BS," I sympathised.

"Right on, then rolled in horseshit and topped with a

dog turd," improvised Red as he cut off another hunk of steak.

~~~~~

I recalled a time I had been travelling in South Asia. In a dusty, crowded railway station, half of which lay in decay, I had encountered a fine example of the hopelessly inadequate bureaucracy that seemed to characterise any meeting with officialdom in that region. I followed an elaborate process of buying a train ticket and attempting to reserve a seat, something that involved my being sent back and forth between several different ticket clerks, queueing afresh each time, and the inspection of a number of archaic ledgers, timetables, fare tables and rule books, none of which appeared pertinent to my journey. The eventual fruit of these endeavours was a third class ticket that was torn from a roll lying on a desk - the desk I had initially visited. Reservation of a seat, I was informed, was not possible any less than three months in advance of departure. I wondered why I could not have been told this at the beginning. The train would be leaving at a quarter past nine in the morning.

I waited the whole day for the train to arrive. The station master, a uniformed, bespectacled gentleman with a moustache and pot-belly, his own manner of projecting gravitas and maintaining the illusion of authority, assured me on at least a dozen occasions that the service would be arriving "in one hour, sir". As night fell and I patiently asked once again regarding the status of the train, he explained politely that there was no train to my destination that day. I suspected that he had known this the whole time, and he said it to me as if it had been self-evident all along – as though our previous conversations had never happened. I questioned whether he knew himself if he was telling the truth or not, so evident was the lack of distinction in his mind between fiction and reality. It was enough to drive any sane person to despair.

Somehow this utter ineptitude, whilst greatly disheartening, I found forgivable. I was about to remonstrate with the station master but then noticed an almost surreal fakeness in his uniform. I remembered stories that Neil had told me when we had been waiting for our battery to arrive in Uganda, of the cargo cults of the South Pacific, marching ingenuously around imitation airstrips and jerry-rigged control towers, carrying straw radios and sticks for rifles in ceaseless attempts to entice planes to appear from the sky – their own form of *programme*. They believed that the rituals in themselves would be sufficient to coax the aircraft from the heavens, bearing wondrous cargo, as they had done in times past when American and Japanese war planes had landed there regularly.

My mood relaxed with the realisation that thus was this station master's own *programme* – one of train-summoning. He believed that his hat, his ledgers, his ersatz uniform, his fiendishly perplexing procedures, his decaying station and his reassurances to his passengers would be sufficient to make the trains run on time. Mysteriously enough, some of them did.

~~~~~

I had overcome my despair at the hands of the station master and could now, years later, look back upon my lost day, spent waiting for a fictitious train, with a smile. What Red was experiencing, however, seemed born of a different origin. It came from a spite of, a contempt for, and most of all, a fear of the ordinary citizen. He would never be able to look back upon this episode with anything other than ill feeling. It bordered on the supernatural that the Byzantine rules he described, the product of some nameless, faceless jobsworth's imagination far back, invisible and intangible, could keep he and Jen from the land of his birth, a tract of the Earth's surface stretching from the Arctic Archipelago to Nova Scotia to Vancouver Island. These laws were the new, dull, elemental forces that persisted over the planet. You could fight them, like you could fight gravity, but you would never rid yourself of them. They grew steadily more sinister as governments grew more fearful of their own people.

Nyree spoke, "But Canada's such a big place! Couldn't you get Jen in from America?"

"*From* America? We're *becoming* America!" laughed Red, shaking his head. "Have you seen how the Midwest US grain-belt and California are burning up and turning to desert? Well, Canada's their backup, they're heading up there like a ferret up a set of pants, for food and, especially, *water*. A lotta places down there, they're having to drill for water like it's oil. They're going *miles* deep with their wells. And this is how messed up it gets – nobody's allowed to collect rainwater. It's illegal. *Illegal to collect water, man!* All the water belongs to the water companies and you have to buy it from them." He sighed to relieve the tension he had built up, then returned to Nyree's question. "No, we thought about it, getting in from the States, but then Jen couldn't work. I'd be breaking the law technically. It could be done but it would make life difficult. We don't need that kind of hassle, man. If we go back, we'll go through their stupid goddam' process and pay. For the moment, we'll sit it out and see what happens following World War Three, that's what's comin'."

"You're right," agreed Joe. "You know Patagonia's looking like a no-go?"

"Ah, snap!" Red cursed. He pretended to bang his fist on the table, laughing. "It's back to yak herding after all, Jen. Sorry, I tried to give you a better life!"

Jen's shoulder's shook lightly as she giggled. "You're coming too?!"

"Y'know, the thing is, *chiquita*," said Red, "I don't know how to break it to you, but I don't want to be a yak herder. As hard as I try, I can't imagine enjoying that."

"Oh! It's OK. You'll have fun. You don't have to keep yaks, there are plenty coal mines!" she joked.

Red smiled nervously and digressed, talking as he was thinking. "Forgive me this brain-fart, but I'm thinking we go to somewhere more, like, a little tropical island with no-one on it, where no-one's gonna screw with you, where no-one's gonna invade you, you can do what you want, it's sunny... Fer chrissakes, look at Canada. It's freakin' huge. *Huge*, man. But any time you go in or out, or move around, or buy somethin', or use the web, or make a call, or use a vehicle, or even carry your phone, they've got you covered. I mean, seriously, man, what the fucking *fuck*? So anyway, on some little island, no-one can touch you. If they do, you just sail away..."

Joe assumed a far-off look. "Or, the boat *is* your island," he said abstractedly.

"What boat?" Red looked confused.

"You said you'd sail away," said Joe. "I'm presuming you're talking about a boat. A boat basically is a floating island. That's pretty genius, Red."

Neil looked shocked. "Wait a minute. Did Red just come up with an idea? What... what's happening?" He turned to Red and held his face up close to him, as though examining him. "Mate, do you need a lie-down after the exertion? Something to top up your brain-sugar?" He belly-laughed and hit him playfully on the shoulder. Red smiled and tried not to show the pain as he clinked glasses with Joe.

Joe went on. "Right. I'm up for the boat idea, I don't know about anyone else. Red's got it right, it doesn't matter if we're in The North of Canada or Southern Patagonia, or wherever. On land, we're subject to the whims and caprices of whatever jobsworths happen to be in charge at the time and the vagaries of wars and politics, like this handbag-waving thing with Chile. There's no escaping, and we won't keep ourselves hidden forever. At sea, on the other hand, we're just seafarers in international waters, we can go where we want and do what we want. In the middle of the ocean, no-one knows and no-one cares. It's so simple, it's beautiful. Redface," he swung his shoulders to face Red, "in a Savant syndrome kind of way, you are a genius. Cheers to Redbeard!"

We drank to Red, who went even redder as he blushed. "Team effort," he said modestly and sipped his beer, then went on, "Y'know, in Korea, quite commonly they'll say the English word 'Fighting!' as a toast. It's one of those funny cases where a word gets adopted from another language, completely out of context. I think they must've just liked the word and the sense of it." He wound himself up, preparing for a rendition. "You've gotta say it like this... *Hwighting!*" he barked.

"Like that!" corroborated Jen.

We all concurred this was an excellent way of cheersing and toasted Red again with a simultaneous and forceful "*Hwighting!*" only disrupted by Neil, who shouted *"DRINKING!"* in an orgy of decibels.

"I don't want to spoil the party," chimed in Tina as she poured out more wine, "but I see two small problemos. We don't want this to turn into another Patagonia, after all, do we Joss?!" She looked directly at me with comic laser eyes.

"Yeah, *Josssss!*" repeated everyone in chorus in what had now become an in-joke whose origins lay in the long drive back from Bariloche to Santa Rosa.

"Numero uno," went on Tina, "we don't have a boat. Numero duo, nobody knows how to sail a boat."

"Ny was in the Navy in Israel!" bellowed Neil. "Weren't you, Ny?!"

Nyree had a mouthful of salad that she finished before answering. "It was military service, I just worked in an office," she blushed.

"Don't believe her!" teased Joe. "They've trained her to do everything. She's a crack Navy Commando! That decides it, Ny. You're our captain. No, our *admiral*."

Nyree put on a face of resignation and Joe backpedalled a little. "Seriously though, sweetheart, they sent you out on boats, no?"

"Yes, Rear Admiral. A bit," she admitted jokingly.

"How many people have you killed?" Neil asked her. "Quite a lot, I'd guess. You've got those killer eyes."

This, once again, elicited Nyree's resigned expression.

"My parents have a boat, in Ancona," interrupted Frederica, "for eight people – we are eight in our family. I can sail. I learned from my father."

"A sail boat?" I asked, then added without thinking, echoing my train of thought, "A motor boat wouldn't suit us, we'd have to rely on fuel."

Freddie gave me a look that indicated I was being

patronising and I winced. "Of course! Sails and two outboard motors," she confirmed.

Neil was surprised. "How come you've never told me that before, Fred? I didn't know you could sail?"

"Yes you do, Neil." Frederica's cherubic smile faltered marginally and she frowned at him. "My father had come from the boat when he visited all of us at the villa and we talked about it. You don't remember?"

"Uh-oh, *someone's* in a lot of trouble..." Joe grimaced and looked down at the table, then added, mock-obsequiously, "*I* remember it, Freddie. I don't think *Neil* does, though."

Neil realised his blunder and worked furiously to rescue himself. "Wait... Your dad... The boat... To be honest, *bella*, I was so nervous about meeting your mother and father that day that I can't remember anything. I was focusing on making the best impression I could, hoping I'd be good enough in their eyes for their most beautiful daughter. It's all a blur in my head. I just remember how happy I was to be there with you, and when you told me they liked me. Do you forgive me, *bambina*? *Bellisima?*" He squeezed her with one arm and kissed a dimpled cheek. She melted.

Neil looked like he had impressed even himself with this spectacular save but didn't hesitate before carrying on. He could barely contain himself he was so excited at the opportunity for mockery that arose from the present situation. I felt it coming.

He took his arm back from Freddie's shoulder and spoke at me. "Let's see, Joss. We need to find a boat. We've got a boat in Italy, for eight people, and there're eight of us. Italy's where half of us have just come from, including two competent sailors. But instead of staying there, we've all travelled halfway around the world to Argentina, where there might be a war, to drive to Patagonia, where it's absolutely bloody freezing, in a camper van." He just sat there looking at me, grinning.

Everyone heeded the cue. "*Jossssssss!*"

"You big loser!" thundered Neil, guffawing and slapping my back.

"I'll get my coat." I said quietly, the laughter of the others ringing around me. My head dropped and I thought of the once and fearless spider, looking at me from the table in front of me with his two good front legs raised. Things would get better, I hoped.

XVIII

We stayed at the grill into the small hours. They kept the place open for us, bringing round after round of coffee and bottles of wine. Everyone liked the boat idea other than Jen, who was unable to swim, but she submitted gracefully to the group decision that we would trade in Little Billie for a yacht, subject to there being life jackets aplenty. I was impressed by Jen's selflessness. It was the product of a childhood spent on the steppe, rather than in cities, perhaps. I knew that Tina's objections would have been stronger had she been in Jen's position. There remained the question of where we would get a yacht, as the pick-up location would double as our embarkation point, and also of how we would equip it and learn to sail it. The Patagonia idea was killed off for good. Even if we could get past the road blocks to get south, nobody wanted to stay in what could potentially become a war zone. Sitting in front of a huge fold-out map of South America and the Caribbean that I had retrieved from the Kombi and laid out on the table, we decided to reconvene at the grill over brunch the next day. There was no sense in setting off until we knew where we were going.

When Tina and I retired to our tent I couldn't sleep. I could hear Neil and Frederica having sex in the Kombi. Even after they stopped, I lay awake suffering awful guilt for having caused everyone to come to Argentina, my mind racing from all of the coffee I had drunk. When I eventually fell into a fitful half-sleep shortly before dawn, my subconscious set about atoning for my error of judgement and started work on our new, nautical adventure. In dreams I floated on a pink ocean in tubs, dinghies and life rafts towards a setting sun that never set. It was like my dream with the geese.

Upon opening my eyes in the late morning, I experienced one of those waking moments of clarity with which I was familiar from my early time as an engineer. My best problem-solving work had always been done while sleeping. This had eventually been brought to an end by corporate-autistic middle managers with Gantt charts who demanded longer hours and unpaid overtime at weekends, killing my creativity, along with my spirit, and holding my mind close to burnout at all times, the way they liked it. To have everything return to me, now, gave me a sense of relief, as though a healing process was almost complete or something I had misplaced had been given back to me. I lay still for a time with closed eyes and meditated as I had used to do often, allowing my eyes to rotate upwards in their sockets until the focal point of my mind's gaze rolled over and faced towards the back of my head. There, instead of seeing the inside of my skull, I looked into deep space, complete with silvery galaxies and stars that never moved, and I floated through it in silence. I was lucky - my mind was often completely empty, devoid of all thought, and it was little effort to still it and reach this state. I stayed there, drifting in space, enjoying the inner calmness that flowed through my being. Slowly and unconsciously, I allowed the message brought to me by my dream to make sense of itself.

~~~~~

Two hours later, after a long lie-in, we found ourselves back at the same big, heavy, wooden table from the night before, with the map out in front of us. Red sat staring at it, chewing on an enormous hunk of meat from a mixed grill that he had ordered.

"How do you eat so much Redface, you fat bastard?" said Neil, darting in and stealing one of his sausages.

Neil knew he was playing with fire, and enjoyed it. He regarded Red as a worthy opponent and liked to skirmish with him. There had been a time, years back, when we had all been skiing in the French Alps. Red had learned to ski as a child in Canada. He was a good ice hockey player and skier and took great pride in both. While we were out on the mountain slopes, he liked to give the rest of us advice on our skiing technique. Neil, unwilling to admit that Red was the best at something, would pretend not to listen. Although a relative novice, he would imperil life and limb to race Red down the slopes or follow him off-piste, leaving Joe and I behind and infuriating Red with his balls-out risk-taking and sheer, headlong stubbornness – something impressive to behold in itself. Neil would then compound Red's ire by giving him mock-serious technique pointers of his own at the bottom of the runs and over dinner in the evenings.

Walking back from a bar in the mountain resort one bitterly cold night, Neil had hit Red in the ear with a well-aimed shot from a snowball. He usually relied on his nimble feet to save him when Red went after him, but on this occasion he had slipped on some ice and Red had caught him. Taking revenge for the days of vexation, Red had hauled Neil to a snowdrift by the side of the road and had sat on him, using his bulk to pin him down, and had then pressed his face into the snow. While we had frozen ourselves just watching the action unfold, there had sat Red, with Neil moaning and yelling, for fully twenty minutes, holding his face in the snow. He had held it there until Neil had finally surrendered to his demands and announced to the assembled crowd of passers-by that Red was by far the better skier, as well as promising several times that he would never question his skiing expertise again. When Red had let him go and he had pulled himself up from the snowdrift, one side of Neil's face had been completely frozen and numbed. He had been worried that it had "died", and he had not been able to move it or open his right eye for a long time after. It was the only time I had ever seen him defeated outright. Despite his complaints, he had seemed exhilarated by the experience of being beaten. Ever since, Red had been his favourite target for jokes.

Red, still chewing on his hunk of meat, now looked at Neil for a few seconds without speaking before, in a tit-for-tat attack, he quickly and deftly took one of Frederica's sausages. Freddie glared at him, but he simply deflected her glare to Neil, who had already taken a bite from the sausage he'd pilfered from Red's plate.

"Give the sausage back to Red, Neil," Freddie ordered. He immediately looked crestfallen.

"I want that hash brown too, man, to make up for the bite of sausage," demanded Red, capitalising on his advantage. "Else this hostage sausage is not getting released."

Neil realised he was in no position to bargain and, trying to maintain his pride as much as possible, returned the sausage to Red along with a hash brown from his plate. Joe looked on approvingly. "Nice hostage taking by Red. Good real-world illustration of the difference between a woman and a terrorist."

Tina's ears pricked up. "Which is?"

"You can negotiate with a terrorist!" Joe delivered the punchline. "Do you think Neil was going to argue with Freddie there? No way!"

Tina rolled her eyes. "Ugh. That's just not funny *at all*. In fact, it's *stupid*. I'm so glad I'm not a man. It must be like being trapped inside the brain of a five year-old."

"Well at least..." began Joe.

Tina immediately cut him out. "Don't even go there, *girlfriend!*" she warned. "It's too early!"

Joe backed down and the four girls exchanged congratulatory glances, smirking. Alongside him and Neil and Red, Tina and the other girls looked immaculate, despite all of the wine we had consumed the previous night. I became conscious of my own, somewhat rough, appearance.

With equilibrium now restored to the universe and to his mixed grill platter, Red's attention turned back to the map, which he eyed intently.

"The Caribbean, it's gotta be, man!" he said to himself after some deliberation. "That's where I am... sun-kissed beaches, palm trees, fruity cocktails, passing out in pools of my own puke..." he laughed.

Tina looked up from her pancake. "Ca-*ri*-bbean, hell yeah!" she enthused. "Able seafarer, Tina B, reporting for duty! When do we haul anchor, or whatever?" This amused Freddie.

Joe waded in. "Right. But won't every sod and his dog on his mega-yacht be floating around the Caribbean, doing the same thing? We won't be the first people to have this idea, just like we weren't the only ones trying to get away to Patagonia, not by a long shot. Yeah, it's a big place, there's no denying, but the small boat traffic there must be quite concentrated, compared to, say, the Atlantic, no?"

"Hm, maybe," offered Frederica, "but it's more important the hurricane season, I think. It's now in the Caribbean, until October. With my father I was in a very big storm once, near Grenada."

Joe's eyebrows raised. "Wow, you're on it, Freddie. You're more of a sailor than you're letting on, am I right?"

Freddie simply hid what she knew behind one of her smiles, but she was good, you could tell. I felt it was my turn to speak. I addressed myself to everyone, but in her general direction, "What does everyone think of this…?"

Neil moaned. "Someone, someone! Please stop him!" he almost yelled. The waiters looked over. "No, mate, we're not going to Antarctica, or… or *Greenland*, or wherever it is you want to take us next. We'll be lucky if we get out of Argentina alive!" He clapped me on the back and cackled through a mouthful of bacon.

I tried to continue what I'd been saying. "STOOOPPP!" Neil exploded, and roared with laughter again. Tina found my evident frustration at trying to speak entertaining.

At the third attempt, I succeeded. "OK, how about this? Do you know about the Kon-Tiki expedition?"

"Yes!" jumped Freddie. There were nods and shakes of the head from the others.

I explained. "Alright, it was like this, essentially: A bunch of mostly Norwegians set out from Peru, from

Lima, on a raft made of balsa, back in the nineteen-seventies. They wanted to show that the islands of the South Pacific could have been first inhabited by people arriving from South America, rather than from Asia, which was the prevailing wisdom at the time. They were pushed all the way to a little island there, I forget which one, by the winds and currents, which move east to west, south of the equator."

Neil looked serious. "Mate, we're not building a balsa wood raft. *Balsa wood?!* You're crazy. STOOOOOOPPPPPP!" he bellowed. Red started laughing and couldn't stop himself.

"That's not what I'm saying," I halted him. "I'm saying we get a boat in Lima. We aim to sail around off the coast of Peru, far enough out that we never bump into anyone. If anything goes wrong - we lose the mast or some other disaster - we end up drifting west to the islands of the South Pacific – it's a backup."

It was this way that I had interpreted the messages being sent to me in my strange dreams, in which I was always moving west towards a setting sun. I wanted to see what the others made of it. There was no immediate chorus of approval, or disapproval.

"As long as we don't get stuck in the Doldrums," said Joe, ominously. From our faces he could see he would have to explain. "On the equator there's a region where it's dead calm, no wind blows. They call it the Doldrums."

"Yes. The Doldrums," Frederica repeated Joe's words, before educating him a little. "But it changes, in some places it is wider than in other places, and it can move with the seasons also."

"And you've got to look out for the Great Pacific

Garbage Patch, don't forget," said Nyree jocularly over her muesli. "We don't want to be running into that."

"No need to worry about that, Ny. We'll steer around it," I joked back flippantly, describing an arc trajectory with my hand.

The Garbage Patch was just one more blot on our dying planet that barely merited a mention. The turtles that died from eating plastic bags, believing them to be jellyfish; the beaches that in years to come would be made up of grains of plastic rather than grains of sand; the rotting carcasses of seabirds on the coasts of remote islands that exposed cigarette lighters and condoms where their stomachs should have been. These were disgraces that remained out of sight and out of the human collective consciousness, along with the flaming tundra, dead coral reefs, disappearing forests, and northern seas boiling with methane that brought in whole tides of poisoned fish.

Neil, to my surprise, began to speak earnestly. "There was some Mexican or Costa Rican guy, José something, a shark fisherman. Something like that happened to him, too. He drifted right across the Pacific. They reckon he ate his crewmate. He was out for over a year, landed on some little island and no-one believed his story. It was vish. I love stuff like that."

"Here we go," said Joe. He had brought the internet set-up along for the session and had the satellite internet hub connected to his phone. "He set sail from the Mexican coast and spent thirteen months at sea before landing in the Marshall Islands. He survived on fish, rainwater and turtle's blood. Doesn't say anything about him eating anyone."

"It is possible," said Frederica. "In the open ocean the fish and turtles gather beneath any object that floats.

Underneath a boat you will see them often. Because of this he could have caught them."

"Sounds like a design flaw in turtles. Do they want to get eaten?" Joe remarked, then held up the phone and showed us a photo of a long-haired, bearded, weathered but surprisingly healthy-looking castaway. "What an absolute legend. We should put him on the legends list."

"You always go on about the legends list, but I've never actually seen it," said Nyree.

"It's on my phone. I'll show it to you."

"That Swedish guy who got snowed in and trapped in his car and hibernated in it the whole winter should be on there," said Red.

"He's on there," confirmed Joe. "Legend."

I proposed a legendary entry. "What about that fisherman in Iceland who swam six hours to an island off the coast when his boat sank and then hiked across the mountains barefoot in the snow to the nearest town?"

"Yeah, Gulli the fisherman, he's on there too. Legend. All the other crew died within a few minutes from the cold. Nobody could understand how he survived. They studied him afterwards and found that his fat was like a seal's. I got interested in that story when I was writing my folklore book. I reckon it goes to show that all those Norse folk tales of the Selkies, the seal people, are basically true."

Tina was interested. "Selkies? What a cool name!"

"Uh-huh. There are Selkie men and women," Joe informed us. "They come ashore sometimes, to dance on empty beaches and in caves. They turn into people by taking off their skins. If a human man can steal a Selkie girl's seal skin, then she'll stay with him and marry him. They'll be happy like that, but she'll spend a lot of time looking longingly out to sea. If she ever finds her skin, she won't be able to resist running away and going back to the ocean forever."

"That's quite sad," said Tina.

"Just like most relationships," opined Joe. "Look at me and Ny, for instance. I used to be able to go away for weekends on the lash with my mates and sleep on beaches and in parks and things, but now she's trying to get me to eat salads and starting to hint that it's time for kids. My life is ruined."

He tried to keep a straight face as he said this but failed and broke into a mischievous chuckle. Tina sucked her teeth and waved a dismissive hand at him, then expressed her condolences to Nyree for having to put up with him.

As if prompted by this, Nyree offered us an idea. "We should just sail to NZ, if we're headed out that way. Then we could stay on my auntie's farm when we arrive."

"If we're going to your auntie's farm, why don't we just fly there?" posited Joe, looking at her.

"Because that's nowhere near as much fun, is it?!" she pointed out.

Tina nodded violently. "Yeah, *this* time, I know it's the end of the world and blah, but can we just make it a holiday rather than some mission to somewhere absolutely freezing? Caribbean or Pacific – if it's sunny with a beach, I'm in!"

"In this case, we must go to the Tuamotus, it's my dream!" said Freddie longingly, looking skyward. These were, we learned from her explanation, a set of tiny, idyllic islands in French Polynesia, famous amongst sailors for their clear waters, technicoloured coral and fish, and great natural beauty.

"Let's hope they're still there when we arrive!" I said, only part-joking, mindful of the plight of the numerous Pacific island nations that were steadily disappearing beneath the waves. Sea level was no longer a constant point of reference, as it had been for cartographers for centuries. In these times, it rose steadily, and the map-makers struggled to keep up.

As if by magic, it was all starting to come together. We agreed that we would sail to New Zealand from Lima if possible, stopping at islands in the Pacific along the way. It was a trip that Frederica had dreamed of since her Caribbean adventures as a teenager with her father, when he had regaled her with tales of coral seas and terrestrial paradises from the sailing odysseys of his youth. She recounted them to us now. All of our apprehensions dissolved as we listened. She was not afraid of our new undertaking. She captivated all of us with her father's stories, inspiring us with visions of the young Italian who, with little sailing experience and a couple of friends, had done everything that we were now planning to do, forty years before, inspired by the maverick early round-the-world yachtsmen.

We decided that we would drive to Lima in Little Billie, taking the route through Bolivia now that the border with Chile was closed. An internet search by Joe uncovered dozens of boats for sale in Lima. As in everywhere else, the economic crisis was forcing people to sell off assets cheaply. We assigned ourselves the roles that we would carry out on the boat. Freddie, who was a certified day skipper, as she eventually revealed, would be skipper. Neil was elected chief engineer, though he preferred the term "first mate". They would choose and procure the vessel. Tina and I would be navigators, with Joe and Nyree on equipment and Red and Jen in charge of supplies, many of which were taken care of already in the Kombi. We set off northwards that same afternoon, keen to leave Argentina behind us as it braced for war.

~~~~~

I felt much more at ease with myself now. I was glad to have contributed something to the new plan but pleased not to be the sole creator of it. As we rolled across the unending plains that bound the long, straight road that points north from Santa Rosa to Córdoba, I dwelt mentally on tales that I had read of the Torres Strait Islanders and aboriginal saltwater peoples of the Great Barrier Reef. In bygone times, they had used long, lyrical songlines to navigate in those seas, and the songlines had been passed down the generations by way of musical recitation and memory. As with the bush trackers on the land, they would have relied on almost invisible signs in the ocean and skies to find their way. I wondered whether the songlines still survived, what warnings they contained, what had happened when fog had descended or when the skies had been obscured. I wondered, even, if the songlines still rang true in the changed oceans. Not long ago, the Torres Strait Islands had been abandoned to rising waters and there were no Islanders living there any more.

I would now, through necessity, be learning of water, wind and skies. I would be observing changes in the ocean and its creatures. I would have to learn to smell land on the wind and to feel the approach of an oncoming storm in the air. I would have to know the clouds, the tides and the currents, and their peculiarities and foibles, just like I knew those of my friends. You do not learn these things from books. There was always so much to learn. This was a new world to explore.

XIX

Three days passed. We sputtered northwards into the mountains from Jujuy towards the Calchaquí valleys, Little Billie struggling up the steep inclines, her engine running on the cheap sugar cane alcohol of the surrounding region. As we distanced ourselves from civilization the Argentine folk laments that reached us on the radio began to crackle and break up, and the signal strength from the cellphone networks faded. Nyree was forced to switch to the satellite internet hub to perform her remote canine Reiki sessions. She would rise very early to catch the middle of the European working day and conduct everything online. She then often slept for some hours once we were on the road after breakfast. She was the only one of us actively bringing in money, though my small income from my investments faithfully continued to trickle in, as did Joe's.

From the Calchaquí valleys we entered the Quebrada de Humahuaca, the high mountain passage that links Argentina with Bolivia. I loved the sound of it, *La Quebrada de Humahuaca*. Ever since seeing it for the first time on a map, I had believed it should be visited just for its name. I kept a collection of places like this in my head and intended to visit them all some day. Some of them I had been to already: Zanzibar, Sulawesi, Ooty, Florianopolis, Skye, Cape Comorin, Tierra del Fuego. There were many others I had yet to visit: The Perfume Mountains, The Never Summer Mountains, The Spice Islands, Madagascar, Curaçao, The Skeleton Coast, Sikkim, Xinjiang, Moab, Hokkaido, Fremantle, The Coral Sea, the Irrawaddy and Orinoco rivers...

The high valley terrain was psychedelic. Multi-coloured mountains of red, lime green, grey, purple and yellow rose around us, and llama roamed amidst giant cacti and dwellings of adobe and concrete. Our weariness and the high altitude, over three thousand five hundred metres above sea level, compounded the hypnotic effect. It seemed as though we were moving through a dreamscape, an ephemeral Xanadu of the imagination that would vanish once the spell was broken.

It was the afternoon. "I'm gonna stop," said Neil, who was driving. "We can camp off the road down here. There'll be a queue to cross the border and I can't be arsed with doing that in the dark."

At that moment, we found ourselves in a wide, flat valley studded with cactus and lined on both sides with high, barren peaks. Ahead of us, in the far distance, we could see a long, snow-capped mountain range. We pulled off the road and put the van in a dry riverbed behind a small hillock. "We'll have to hope it doesn't rain," observed Neil.

We set up the tents near the van, weighing them down with stones on the dry, rocky ground. The air was perfectly still. Red disappeared and came back carrying the wood from a dead cactus, which was cylindrical, grey-brown in colour and perforated with holes like a giant honeycomb. We heard his footsteps crunching towards us from a long way off.

"This place is freakin' weird, man. Can you imagine living here? It's a desert!" Red said as he arrived.

"I can imagine it," said Jen, who looked the most at ease of all of us in this place. "If the llama can live here, the people can live here also."

Hearing conversation, Joe emerged from the back of the Kombi holding a book. It was clear he was about to illuminate us with something he'd read. Sure enough, he began to lecture.

"It looks like a desert around here, but a lot of these empty peaks have old Inca ceremonial sites on them. They've found remains of human sacrifices on quite a few. The bodies get preserved perfectly by the cold and the dryness. A lot of the corpses had miniature replicas of themselves with them, dressed in exactly the same clothes and hats, and with little llamas, all made of seashell, or silver, or gold. Their souls were meant to enter the figures to pass into the spirit world."

"Ha. What a bunch of goddam' hippies!" Red retorted.

~~~~~

In the Alpujarra in Spain, on the southern slopes of the Sierra Nevada, a dry, deserted landscape stretches to the horizon. I had walked through it for days. To my surprise, in steep ravines and gullies hidden in dead ground, I had found orchards of apricot and peach, tomatoes and olive groves, even villages of whitewashed homes with terracotta roofs. While I could not see it now, I felt that this high Argentine valley would be the same. The bleak villages and small signs of life that we had seen from the road were just an inkling of why the people of this place had chosen to live here. It was a place that had its own hidden magic, I was sure, and Jen saw it more clearly than me.

Red and Jen were getting a smoky fire going, using the abundant dry llama dung as well as cactus wood, as the sun dropped behind the mountain, still an hour or so from nightfall. Freddie was going through some boxes of food, deciding what to cook that evening. Neil paced around her.

"I'm not eating tins again," he said to nobody in particular, a restless look on his face. "Who wants something fresh?"

"A'righhht, now you're talking," tuned in Joe. He was already sizing up the llamas that seemingly roamed free around the area.

Nyree clocked what they were thinking straight away. "You can't, you two!" she pleaded.

"We've got to learn to fend for ourselves, Ny." Joe walked over to where she was, near the fire, and faced her, putting his forearms on her shoulders.

"But we'll never eat a whole one. It's cruel!" she protested.

Neil moved over from the van and joined them, to tell a story. "When I was guiding in Botswana there was a night when a lion came and killed seven zebras close to our camp. It was a slaughter. We went over to look and see what had happened the next morning and found all the dead zebras lying there, like they hadn't been touched. But listen," he went on, "when we looked closer we saw that the only bits he had eaten were the *genitals*. He did the same thing a few other times after that, too, deviant bastard. We called him 'The Gourmet'."

Nyree looked at him like she was going to become tearful. "What's your point, Neil?"

"Nature is cruel, but nothing's ever wasted," he stated. "The hyenas and the vultures got those zebs. What we don't eat here, the foxes will, or the birds, or the pumas, or even the insects. They have to live, too."

"But these llamas belong to someone. Look, they've got little woollen tassels in their ears." Nyree was still unhappy.

"Do they?" asked Neil rhetorically. "Listen, Ny, they won't miss one, we'll make it a small one. We'll be out of the country and into Bolivia tomorrow morning, anyway, no-one'll know."

Neil walked over to a cactus in the twilight and came back, then looked over at where I was standing, alongside Red and Jen at the fireside. "Redface, Josster, come on." He beckoned us with one hand and held out an array of cactus spikes in the other.

"What's this for?" Red asked as he stood up from the fire and swaggered over, watched by Jen.

"To see who kills the llama, you muppet. Get with the programme." Neil held the spikes up to him and he took one. Joe took his and I took mine, leaving Neil holding the last one.

We held them out. I'd drawn the short spike.

"Josster! You win!" Neil congratulated me. "Don't worry, mate, I'll help you."

I glanced over at Tina, who had congregated with Freddie and Nyree. She looked unimpressed and was sympathising with Nyree. I looked back at Neil, whose blue eyes tunnelled right into me. There was no arguing, I was going to have to kill a llama, so I got on with the job. I would deal with any consequences later. I fetched a length of rope from the Billie-wagon and switched my shorts for jeans and my flipflops for boots and socks, donning my canvas jacket as well to protect my elbows. I took my knife from my bag, a magnificent bone-handled hunting knife of German make that I'd purchased in Brazil, and had not yet used.

"Lasso?" enquired Neil, seeing the rope. Yeah. He and Joe nodded approvingly and the three of us set off towards a group of llamas grazing in the near distance. Their curiosity was aroused by our approach, but they continued about their business of foraging for tufts of vegetation in the sparse brush. I chose a nearby cactus and tied one end of the rope around the base, tying the other end into a lasso. From the collection of llamas, I singled out the animal closest to where I stood, a chestnut brown individual of my height with bright pink woollen tassels through both ears. It eyeballed me while ruminating hurriedly on a scrap of thorny shrub. Without losing its gaze I walked up to it smoothly and swiftly, throwing the big loop of rope up and over its head in the same movement. It read my intention too late, bolting just before the rope touched its neck. This caused the rest of the small herd to run.

"First time! I thought you'd spook him!" Neil whooped.

"Me too," I shouted back, my heart racing. "I figured I'd try my luck for the easy catch!"

The rope suddenly yanked taut around the cactus as it reached its limit, and the llama began to buck in circles at the other end, perhaps twenty five yards away. I hurried towards it, holding the rope as I did so to prevent the animal from running away to either side.

"Get its legs!" advised Joe.

Both he and Neil moved with surprising alacrity, and they were alongside me when I reached the creature. It faced us, snorting and pulling backwards on the rope desperately, causing the noose to start sliding up towards its head. Joe wrapped his arms around the long neck and Neil and I grabbed a front leg each, below the shoulder. I could smell the llama's breath and its musty coat of wool. Its back legs kicked wildly, sending dust into the air which went into my eyes and mouth. With a heave and a lift we brought it down on its side, still struggling violently.

"Do it quickly!" Neil panted.

Joe was kneeling with one knee at the top of its neck. He slid down to the base as I moved from the shoulder to the head of the creature. I pushed with the weight of my knee just behind its skull. Adrenaline pumped through my veins and I consciously rushed, not allowing time to question myself. I drew the knife from its sheath on my belt and pressed the point of it hard into the soft hollow behind the llama's ear, pushing the blade all the way through its neck and out of the other side. The large, dark, beautiful eye of the creature watched me as I did so, the last of the daylight reflected in the pupil, dilated with fear. I felt the muscles in the neck go very tense as it kicked furiously, then it gave a huge sigh and the kicks became weaker. Jets of bright red blood shot from the knife wound, covering all of us. We kept our weight on the body until it stopped moving.

"Good work," said Joe, completely unfazed by the experience. "That was clean."

"Nice one, mate," echoed Neil.

"Easier than I thought. It wasn't the hardest quarry to out-guile," I replied, gripping the handle of the knife hard to prevent my hand from shaking and trying to hide the tremble in my voice. The fading light hid the tears in my eyes, I hoped. I cursed myself gently for how soft I had allowed myself to become and withdrew the knife from the llama's neck.

In a terrifying moment, it dawned upon me that it was not so easy to quit the *programme*. The slaughter of a domesticated, unsuspecting creature in the most straightforward of circumstances had reduced me to tears. Many, far harsher, realities stood along our way, and I suddenly questioned if I could make the journey. I recalled my youth and how I had taught myself to live, but realised I had only taught myself to live within the confines of the *programme*. There was no denying that it had given me a wealth of things, but I had unwittingly grown up to depend on it, and in doing so had allowed it to take from me that most vital thing of all - my independence.

In all my life and travels, I had never been independent of the *programme* for a moment, aside from that night I had spent as a small child, wrapped in my father's shirt and jumper, on the rocky Cornish beach where my parents had been swept away. I was now letting it go and losing everything it had given me. Out here, in a premonition of what it would be like when the *programme* was gone, the hard-won lessons of my life counted for little. These thoughts struck me sideways, though they should have been nothing new. The act of killing a living creature had been the catalyst that had brought the significance of these truths crashing into my consciousness with the shattering force of a comet. I could not stop the fear welling up within me, but I managed to hold it back. The image of the once and fearless spider flashed across my mind. *What are you afraid of?* I knew that it was not death – that was certain. If there was anything to fear, I realised, it was the *programme* itself, the very thing from which we were escaping. The uncertain road ahead of us, though it would bring hardship, was no more frightening than that of going home to the broken system from which we had come. The fear I felt was a surge of emotion in the face of the Herculean scale of the challenge ahead, and a final sense of the loss of the connection with my home. It was the fear of making the journey across the abyss to independence. The journey began here. The slaughter of this llama was my first, faltering, baby step along it. I would have to teach myself to live again and become independent. I must begin the search for that part of my spirit that had led me, as a child, to huddle for warmth amongst the rocks on the beach in Cornwall – that remnant of my independence which had not been lost to the *programme* and to a misdirected world.

We rolled the animal onto its back, cut the windpipe and removed the genitals, then slit its belly from bottom to top. We heaved out the entrails, reaching up into the rib cage to pull out the heart, lungs and windpipe before cracking the strong sternum, with difficulty, using the knife. By the light of our head torches Neil carefully cut out the fillets from either side of the inner backbone, removing the taut membranes that surrounded them first. Joe and I stood either side of the carcass, keeping the legs and chest splayed apart for him to perform the butchery. Joe insisted we keep the liver, saying it was good for us, and ate part of it fresh. Other than that, and the fillets, we left the rest of the carcass and the entrails for scavengers.

"That meat would need to hang for a few days to be good to eat anyway," reckoned Neil.

~~~~~

With nowhere to wash, we returned to the camp site resembling something from a horror film. I tried to use the darkness to hide from Tina, but she followed me into our tent. When she saw me, she started to cry. Of all of us that evening, Tina was hit hardest by the kind of mental turmoil and self-doubt that I had experienced in the moments after killing the llama. She was the most normal of us, or rather the least mis-fit of our band of misfits. Because of that, perhaps, she was the most tied to the *programme*, and stood to lose the most. She was scared, and angry at what she described as our lack of concern for the 'little people', whose llama we had killed. I listened to her. I could not hold her on my shoulder, with all the half-dried blood that covered me. We promised that we would talk about things, but time was short and we had to hurry to help prepare the dinner. The emotional release that came from expressing her feelings had helped to calm her mind. I wiped the tears from her eyes before she left the tent to re-join the others.

As hunger took over, it was remarkable how quickly the initial atmosphere of shock and unease passed. When we had cleaned the blood from ourselves, and the llama fillets and liver were ready to cook, everyone seemed quite impressed - even Nyree and Tina. After the brief excursion into uncharted territory, we were back inside our comfort zone. Frederica sliced the llama fillets into steaks and began to barbeque them on the embers of the fire. She fried onions from the bag we kept in the van, using them to make a delicious-smelling onion gravy with mustard to go with the liver. The llama killing was soon forgotten.

"Make my first one rare, plenty pepper!" Red called to no-one in particular as he walked through the darkness to the camp fire to eat. He settled himself onto a flat rock that he had carried over himself just for that purpose. The rest of us sat on the ground. "Alright, man! Llama steaks with llama liver, and onions. All done on a llama dung barbeque! Anyone for llama? I can see what you mean now, about the llamas, and all," he said to Jen, who was cross-legged next to him.

"Yes," she said softly. "It's the same in Mongolia, just with yaks." Her dark eyes twinkled with the glow of the fire beneath the starlit sky.

XX

These evenings around camp fires were the best. Everyone always had to tell a story. It could be a new one or one that had been told before. Some of the old ones were the most loved, and they got better with each retelling. Part of the art was to add a new embellishment or two each time you told it, to keep it alive, no matter that it was now an outrageous caricature of the original. The more outrageous it was, the better. There was limitless artistic licence and the truth would never take precedence over a good story. Most of the tales were still new to Frederica, so we were enjoying a nostalgic phase of returning to old classics. Having eaten our steaks and liver, we sat around the fire with beers that we had brought with us from Jujuy. They were cool from having been left on the ground.

It was Nyree's turn to start the storytelling on this occasion and she treated us to a new one. She told us of the time following her national service in the Israeli Navy, after which she had left Israel and gone back to New Zealand, where she had been born. A year or so after returning, she had taken a job in a remote weather station on the top of a mountain with a Kiwi boyfriend, Aaron. The hut in which they lived was powered using solar panels, giving them a limited supply of electricity each day and soon leading to domestic strife. "All he wanted to do was play video games," she told us. "I'd catch him playing them secretly. Essentially, there was enough electricity each day for one hot shower, which was my luxury, or an hour of video games, which was his. We worked out a system where we'd trade. Some days he could have his and some days I'd have mine. One day I'd been out walking, I used to go for walks around the mountain sometimes to exercise and see the kea, clever little birds, real characters, there were whole flocks of them living up there and they'd follow me around wherever I went. Aaron had been out fixing a communications mast, but when I got back he was there in the hut, playing video games, and there was no hot water for the shower. This was, like, the third or fourth time it had happened on my day and I couldn't believe it, I was just *mad*. You know what I did? I picked up the console, went straight back outside and threw it down the mountain. It came from nowhere, I didn't know I had it in me."

This evoked a spontaneous cheer from everyone. "Then what happened?" asked Neil, now hooked.

"You wouldn't believe it, but he actually started *crying*. I'm not even making it up," said Nyree. "I realised, right then, that he loved his video games more than me. In summary, the next day, I headed down off the mountain, on my own."

Neil guffawed. "Good on you, Ny. It's a good story. Next time it could maybe do with a bit more beating of Aaron around the head with a shoe before you throw the computer off the cliff. Or he could throw himself down the mountainside trying to save it, then get eaten alive by the kea as he lies maimed on a ledge." Neil lay on the ground, groaning and acting out being eaten by kea.

"Ha, I'll work on it," she said, "but this first time I, like, just wanted to tell it like it was. On to you, Neil," she nominated him for the next tale.

Neil sat up and chose a simple, scatological fable from his time in Africa. Relieving himself in a bush one day he had, unknowingly, splattered the back of his shorts and shirt with shit. "I had a pretty bad case of the explosive trots, and I was *properly* spattered from bounce-back, all up my back and over my shorts," he recalled. "Nobody told me. We were in this village and all these kids started following me, all pointing and laughing. I thought they found me funny, so I played along and started doing these comic chimpanzee routines and impressions of different animals."

He got up, and performed a chimp act that had us all in stitches. Already, Red had gone into uncontrollable fits of deep laughter, this story tickled his humour to the core. I could picture, in my head, the scene in the village. Neil sat himself down again and carried on.

"I'm telling you seriously, these kids were literally *dying* with laughter. There was one kid I thought had actually died laughing. He'd laughed so long and hard he was just lying there on the ground, not moving. He'd blown his funny fuse. And of course I was there convinced that I was a comedy genius, I was chuffed they found me so funny. I was considering setting myself up as an entertainer and going round all the villages doing shows for kids. It was only hours later that one of the kids' mums pointed out to me that I had shit all up my back, and that's why they were all laughing at me. After that, they all called me poo-man."

"They were pretty much spot on, then, poo-man,"

remarked Joe. Red was still laughing interminably in the background. Neil chuckled and nominated his brother for the next story.

Joe regaled us with an outdoor adventure that had occurred while he was camping in France during university holidays with his ex-girlfriend, Fiona, she of the hair-straighteners. She was a student of engineering at that time, and had inadvertently turned their gas cylinder stove into a rocket whilst trying to set it up for cooking, firing it up into the roof of Joe's tent and burning the whole thing down.

"She was an *engineering* student, can you believe it?" Joe recounted. "There were two stoves. She was boiling water on one and changing the cylinder of the other right next to it. She didn't fit the cylinder properly the first time and took it out to try again, but it was already pierced, and when the gas caught, the canister shot into the roof of the tent like a rocket. I was doing some washing up in a stream, and when I saw the fire I ran over and threw the whole tub of water, with all the cups and pots and everything, onto it. There was a half-drunk glass of orange juice on the ground, which I desperately threw on there as well. Luckily she got out of the tent before it burned down, but it was destroyed and most of our stuff was burned, too. I tried not to lose my cool, but we were in these woods and it was a massive pain in the ass to lose the tent. I was trying to think of what we should do. Anyway, this is the unbelievable thing... *then she started hitting me with a stick!* She picked up this branch from the floor and started beating me with it, yelling that she was going home. Then she just ran off into the woods on her own. She came back hours later. She never apologised or replaced the tent. She just complained that I hadn't shown her how to change the gas cylinder."

After all these years, I thought, he was still a bit hung

up on that girl. It was funny how it happened sometimes. I chuckled at the story.

"She was crazy?!" stated Freddie, questioningly.

Joe nodded. "At least a nine on the Barkometer. That's a scale of one to ten of how barking mad someone is. When I say 'someone', I mean chicks. It's an exponential scale, a bit like the Richter scale. To be a ten you have to be a certified lunatic, but I don't think she was far off."

"That must be like the Wanker Scale for men, then," retaliated Tina humorously. "That goes from fifty to one hundred, because there's no lower range. That's exponential, too."

"Ah," said Frederica, content with both Joe's and Tina's explanations. "What am I on the Bark-ometer?" she asked Neil.

"Oh, you're cool, Freddie, only, maybe, a seven," grinned Neil. She feigned a hurt look and they both huddled a little closer to the fire.

~~~~~

Freddie went next with her story, a recent one from their holiday together in Italy. "One evening we went out to a small *ristorante* in the next village to eat, instead of to cook our own meal. All through the evening, the waiter kept looking at me, and he was quite handsome, I think," she smiled, picturing the scene to herself. "We had a very nice meal. Then at the end, he comes to us to give us our bill, but before that he gives me a flower and asks me for my number, even though he can see I am with somebody else, with Neil. Then, straight after, he gives the bill to Neil."

"It was *ridiculous*," said Joe, who had been there with them as well, along with Nyree.

Freddie continued. "So, we decided to play him a joke, because he is so rude, and very arrogant! We paid the bill with cash, and I left a number between the notes, to make him think he is lucky. But really it is the number of Neil's phone. Each time the waiter calls, Neil gives his phone to me to talk to him, and each time he sends a message, Neil replies. So we arrange that I will meet him one day in a park in the village with the *ristorante*. I am waiting for him there and he arrives, but very, very smart, with clothes and shoes that look new and very expensive. He has a big bunch of flowers, and when he sees me he gives them to me and tries to kiss me. But, *then!*" she began to laugh, thinking back to it, "Joe and Neil are behind him. They were hiding behind some trees, and they pick him up on their shoulders and carry him on to some grass. He is shouting all the time, but there is nothing he can do because he is not so strong, like them. It is *very, very funny*. Then, they take off all of his clothes, and his shoes. He has nothing left to do, so he has to run home, completely naked, in the daytime!"

"And you forgot to mention, Freddie, the most important bit. He had a tiny willy," Neil reminded her.

"Yes, it's true," she confirmed.

"Revenge is sweet," chuckled Neil, "and there are a lot of ways to tell someone to chuff off. It was much better than spoiling that night at the restaurant by lamping the cheeky bastard, or complaining to his manager."

This happy story got a full round of applause and appreciative foot-stomping on the ground. It was difficult to follow.

It fell to me. I popped open another bottle of beer with a cigarette lighter and threw another lump of cactus wood onto the fire, deciding to stay on the theme of public nakedness.

On my eighteenth birthday, completely drunk, my school colleagues had stripped me of all my clothes in the street outside of the pub as we left, a pretty standard routine for an eighteenth birthday. I escaped wearing nothing but my socks and, quickly regaining my sobriety as I was pursued by a few of my classmates down the street, was forced to run home. It lay a couple of miles out of town, down a long country lane. Without any keys to let myself into the house, it dawned upon me that I was going to have to wake up my grandmother when I got back. Wishing to spare her an unwelcome surprise, I decided that I needed at least some form of preserving my modesty for the moment that she opened the front door. It was at that moment that I saw an unsuspecting member of the public coming down the lane towards me in the distance, illuminated by a solitary street lamp that stood outside of another house on the lane. I ducked into the darkest shadows, in the hedge at the side of the road, and waited for his approach. "This bloke had had a few himself," I remembered aloud. "He caught sight of me as I jumped out into the road and he just froze, a bit startled. I was, like, 'Give me your shirt!' It was a mugging, I suppose. But he looked quite relieved, like he'd been expecting worse. He took off his jacket, pulled his shirt off, over his head, and handed it to me. He said 'Here you are, mate.' put his jacket back on, and carried on walking. I suppose he'd seen it all before. I tied the shirt around my waist and ran off in the opposite direction, my bum winking in the moonlight. My first, and only, mugging!"

"Hurray!" said Tina. "What did your gran say when she saw you."

I didn't really want to recall that part of the narrative. Predictably, my grandmother had been none too pleased with my beer drinking, nor with my rite of passage, and hadn't spoken to me for a week.

"Well, it all proved too much for her sensibilities and she had a heart attack and popped her clogs right there on the spot, bless her little soul," I improvised.

"First mugging, and first time frightening a granny to death!" Tina concluded. "Right, I'll go next."

Tina often felt embarrassed that, in her opinion, she didn't have many funny stories. Whenever she told one, though, it was always done in a way that warmed the heart. This time she gave us an anecdote from her childhood, telling of the time when, as a small girl, she had liked fish fingers so much that she used to take them from the freezer and hide them under her bed so that nobody else, particularly her brother, would eat them.

"I must have had ten boxes of fish fingers down there. At least ten boxes, probably more like fifty!" she smiled, getting into the swing of the exaggeration. "I used to check they were still there before I went to sleep each night. I'd always ask for fish fingers for dinner as well, and my mum would never be able to work out what was happening to them all. I was too young to know why they were kept in the freezer and it didn't take long for Mum to find out what was going on. After a couple of weeks, my room *stank* – it smelt like a cesspool full of dead fish, and skunk juice, and sick."

"You haven't completely gotten rid of the lingering rotting sick smell even to this day!" I cracked. She rolled her eyes.

Next came Jen, nominated by Tina. She gave us a

glimpse into another world. A Korean friend of hers had been preparing to marry her Scottish fiancé, a man named Dougie with whom she had been together for three years, and had visited a fortune teller to learn whether theirs would be an auspicious marriage. She was distraught to learn that the union would be extremely unlucky. Not knowing what to do, and unwilling to discuss it with Dougie, she had visited the same fortune teller, an old woman, a second time for advice. This time the old woman had given her a list of names, telling her that if she changed her name, Li-Na, to one of the names on the list, then she could be sure that fortune would favour the couple. After some deliberation over the list, she chose Hyo-Rin as her new name. She told Dougie that she had changed her name for their marriage and asked him to call her by the name of Hyo-Rin from that day on. "He thought she was joking," Jen explained. "He just kept calling her Li-Na. It was very strange for him to call her anything else. Can you imagine? But she was very upset every time he called her Li-Na, and she cried. He didn't understand why. It was only when she said that she could not marry him that he began to call her Hyo-Rin."

"And now?" asked Joe.

"Now they are married and everything is OK," Jen summed up. "So, you see, fortune teller was right. If Dougie had not changed and started to call her Hyo-Rin, they would never have been married!" She giggled.

"Nice logic!" said Joe admiringly.

"It's a true story, man. That kind of thing actually happens quite a bit in Korea," Red told us. It was his turn to round off the storytelling. Everyone looked forward to Red's stories, and this one did not disappoint. Red had spent some time in the Canadian military and chose a tale of when he had been on exercise in the Mediterranean with the United Nations. There, they had been assigned a French drill sergeant who was universally despised as an emotionally repressed, angry, miniature Hitler. "One time we were on drill, and this drill sergeant was acting a real asshole, worse than usual. So as he was walking up the line someone just shouted out *'Wanker!'* just like that. He didn't know who'd done it. He was always angry, man, but this time he just went totally ape-shit, *ape-shit*, running up and down, screaming that we'd all pay for it until he found out who'd said it, and this, and that. He builds himself up to this big crescendo of fury."

At this point, Red put on his French accent, honed from living near the Quebec border for most of his life.

"You ferking maggots, you stinking ass'oles! Putain! You zink I know ferk NUZZING? Eh? Wrong! You miserable, useless, ferking peasants! Eh? I KNOW FERK ALL!" Red went on, "Man, we couldn't stop ourselves, it was just too good. We died laughing at that point, and him just losin' it even more, we just din't care. *Man*, that guy was a bastard."

It was a fitting end to the story telling. Neil explained the punchline to Frederica, who snickered when she had understood. There was much merriment and many cries of *"I KNOW FERK ALL!"* and *"I KNOW FERK NUZZING!"* into the night in our finest French accents. The beer supply was nearly exhausted and Joe went to fetch the whisky.

XXI

Joe returned to the fire with the bottle of cheap whisky that we had picked up in Jujuy and poured it into plastic cups. The discussion at this point turned more philosophical.

"Why don't we care what's happening at home?" said Tina. "Why are we here instead of trying to do something to help where we live?"

"I see it like this," began Joe, passing her a cup. When he resumed talking, he looked as if he was airing a complaint.

"Imagine you're with some chick who you've been with for years, but who suddenly feels she has to start reading all of your messages and emails."

"Like Fiona, of the hair straighteners?" I hazarded a guess.

Joe shot me a look of surprise, like he had not been abstract enough with his words to cover his thoughts. He moved on.

"That on its own is enough to tell you that you have to leave her. But then, on top of that, she becomes the chick from hell. She starts blaming you for things you haven't done, setting you pointless and near-impossible tasks, like the twelve tasks of Hercules, taking all of your words out of context and holding them against you, even if you can't remember ever saying them, wasting all your money, wasting all your time, getting suspicious about who you're talking to and spending time with, blaming you for things you haven't done, blaming you for things that *she* hasn't done..."

"That's, what? A nine on the Barkometer?" I queried.

"Eight point five," corrected Joe.

"But I was a seven!" protested Frederica.

"It's exponential, Freddie, seven is a lot lower than eight point five," Joe reassured her, then joked, "I'm sure Neil was just joking, in any case. I'd put you at six point five."

"Pah!" Frederica dismissed him with a hand.

"In a nutshell, you'd have to have no self-respect whatsoever to put up with someone that bonkers. Only the most emasculated, lily-livered excuse for a bloke would take it, no matter how good the BJs - sorry, Freudian slip – I mean, *benefits*, are," Joe went on.

That was why he put up with Fiona for so long, perhaps, I thought to myself.

"Bee-Jays?" questioned Freddie.

Joe blushed, unusually for him. "Sorry, Freddie. By

BJs, I mean the *good* parts of the relationship. I'll leave it to Neil to translate the exact meaning," he advised.

"Oh, thanks, brother," responded Neil.

Joe waited.

"Oh, you're actually serious." Neil straightened himself and pondered something. "Well, let me tell you what an old Afrikaans guy said to me when I was in Botswana. It's a little rough, in the 'Kaans way, so I apologise - be prepared." Freddie nodded.

Neil put on a well-practised South African accent, slow and with pauses and much emphasis, and started his recital. "Mark mai words, bru. If there is one thing Ai tell you, it is this – Do not marry just a *snatchbox*. She must 'ave something ilse! Maybe she can *cook*. Maybe she 'as a sense of *'umour*. Maybe... she is a liddle bit *intelligint*. You know? But there must be *something*. Too many okes are stolen away by the *snatchbox*. Then they are *lost*. There 'as to be something ilse."

Neil paused and dropped the accent. "So, when Joe says 'BJs', he really means all of those good things that the old Saffer was talking about: having a good sense of humour, being intelligent, being a good cook... all that stuff." I smiled at how gentle Neil was with Freddie. She nodded again and Neil winked at Joe as the signal to carry on.

Joe put his discourse back on track. "So, in short, you decide to leave this crazy, impossible girl. You have to, it's as simple as that. But, here's the catch. That chick is *the government*. You *can't* leave her."

"Can't leave her? She's, like, an enchantress or something?" Red questioned.

Joe nodded. "In one, Red, she's a *wicked witch*. Who you can never leave! So you have to *kill* her." His story-telling side was coming out. "In our case, we're lucky, we've got people handling the situation for us. That's what all those kids back home are doing at the moment. They're burning the witch at the stake. *Which* allows *us* to observe from a safe distance, with *steaks*, at minimal inconvenience to ourselves. I don't know about you, but that's why I'm here."

"That's completely selfish!" said Tina.

"I don't think so," Joe shook his head. "Look, there are eight of us. That's about the same size as a family. We're all helping each other. Everyone brings their own thing. Joss takes us on outrageous detours of thousands of miles to war zones, my brother's a nob, Ny regularly ear-bashes me, Red's a semi-literate Canadian peasant, and so forth." He had amused himself at this point, and stopped to laugh.

"Anyway, this way I'm helping myself and seven other people. And I've helped mum out with a few things remotely." Joe looked over at Neil. "If everyone did the same, then things wouldn't be that bad."

"But the thing is," he went on, "that's not really the *point*. The point is that it's impossible to trust someone who doesn't trust you. It has to work two ways. If this hypothetical wicked witch stops all the craziness and paranoia, you're just left with the *benefits*, and shortly enough thereafter, *magically*, all is forgiven, or forgotten. Problem is, you're never going to change her – you'll waste your life trying, and probably get dragged down with her and turn into what you hate. A toad, maybe. She has to transform *herself*. If she trusts another person, then they'll trust her."

"Hell, man, I don't even trust myself!" complained Red.

"If I was you, Red, I wouldn't either," Joe grinned. "Anyway, in conclusion, Tina, to answer your question. I'm here to escape this nightmare chick from hell, this wicked witch. I'd be happy in a relationship where I was trusted as a starting premise, but she spies on me and treats me like a bastard. If I'm treated like a bastard, I might as well be one, it makes no difference. So here I am..."

"Being a bastard?" Tina finished for him, laughing.

He reflected as the analogy began to fail, and dropped it. "Basically, I'm just not *invested* any more. With all this secret, so-called *security* apparatus, that they can screw you with, without being accountable, they've fathered the beast that's eating them now... a generation that hates them because they've raped it. It's grown up outwitting them on a small scale, and it's grown-up enough now to outwit them on a grown-up scale. A lot of people's entire lives have become a kind of contest of wits against an unseen adversary. The authoritarian state might dominate for a while, until enough people wake up and join in, but no system will win against the combined intelligence of tens of millions of brains, never. Now it's happening, and it's *them*, the *elite*, ha, that have something to fear, because they've got *a lot* to hide. I say bring it on."

"The bizarre thing is," he added as an afterthought, "you *do* get a lot of people who put up with all that grief, the wicked witch scenario. The propensity of people to endure things, just through inertia and habitual routine, is incredible. How many paranoid, unhappy marriages have you seen like that? Same with the system — there're people back home who're still following their standard routines, turning up to work and acting like everything'll be fine again one day if they just carry on, putting up with things, same as ever."

"Government cannot trust everybody, Joe, there are always bad people," pointed out Jen.

"You're right, Jen, but they always used to be able to deal with the bad ones without having to spy on all the decent ones - that is, nearly everyone - as well. It's a problem for government to solve, not my problem. Listen, when I sit down to write a private message to somebody, I have to self-censor what I put in it, because I know the plods are reading it. They can kiss my chuddies, and then go and kiss their own. *They've killed the spirit of the internet.* I'm a trustworthy person, I shouldn't have to do that. It's bordering on thought control. It *is* thought control."

Red looked impressed. "You should go for Prime Minister or somethin', man."

Joe snorted in disgust. "Politics is a waste of time. There are enough massive egos and psychopaths around to do that admin job for all of us. After this lot are brought down, which they will be, I guarantee there'll be a new band of hot-shot muppets to run the show, all 'different' from the last lot... yeah, right. It's like wrestling. The contest's a charade to keep the peasants happy – the outcome's already decided. Meantime, I'm sitting around camp fires eating steaks and drinking whisky, a way more productive way to spend my existence."

"*Now* you sound selfish!" reiterated Tina light-heartedly.

Joe grinned to himself, sipping his whisky. "Alright, maybe just a bit, but it's more fun that way. Besides, we *are* the 'me' generation..."

His discourse over, Joe lay back flat on the ground

and studied the desert sky, showered with stars.

I began to sip my whisky, too. I loved these times. It was these kind of conversations that, I supposed, I wished I had been able to have with my mother and father while growing up, if they had been alive.

"One thing you've forgotten, Joe," I said.

"What's that?"

"No matter what the chick from hell does, even if she stops being crazy overnight. Even if she, very hypothetically," I added dramatically, "bottoms out at *zero* on the Barkometer..."

"Impossible," interrupted Joe, "The best you can hope for is a chick that *admits* that she's bonkers."

"Well, imagining..." I continued, "even if all that happens, she can't stop the planet from overheating. That's why I'm here, because everything pales into insignificance alongside that. Did you see about that super-typhoon that just hit Japan? It was a storm the size of *India*, category five, that engulfed the whole country. It's awful, I hate to think what it's done there. I agree with you on the politics, but it's child's play compared to what Mother Earth has in store for us."

Joe murmured something. As usual, nobody wanted to talk about the state of the Earth. Its coming fate was something that most people, even my closest friends, were either resigned to, or ignored, like death itself, or the weather. I changed the subject.

"You know," I said, "the Inca constellations weren't made of stars. They used the dark parts of the sky. Do you see the llama?" I pointed to a black region amongst the glittering stars above the outline of a peak on the horizon.

If you looked closely you could see the silhouette of a llama. I had come across these features during my reading into navigation by the night sky. "There's an eagle too, somewhere," I said, scanning the heavens for it unsuccessfully.

"Ha," said Joe, diverted. "You see, Ny. The llama went up to the sky. Look. I can see his pink woollen tassels."

We all looked up at the llama in the sky. At this altitude, the stars appeared hard and sharp, like millions of splinters of ice, though they burned with eternal fire. I apologised to the llama for having killed him.

~~~~~

Nyree now spoke, returning to the theme of selfishness. "A lot of people are afraid to be selfish. They're afraid of freedom." She was smoking a joint that Neil had rolled for her and had lit on the fire.

Neil was rolling another joint for himself. "We've gotta smoke all this stuff before we get to the border," he muttered.

"That doesn't make sense," Tina replied to Nyree.

"Actually, it does, T, but I know it sounds weird at first. If you're free it means you can do what you want. That's, like, the definition of freedom. If you can do what you want it means that *you*, only you, are responsible for wherever your life is at. A lot of people aren't happy with their lives, but they can't accept that it's their fault, and that they have the freedom to change it if they want. They want to blame something else, or someone else. It happens with dogs, too."

"With dogs?" Tina looked surprised at the

introduction of this new thread to the discussion.

"Yeah, think. Sometimes dogs are not happy. Perhaps they're mistreated, or they just don't like their owner, or they're terrorised by children in the house. If they really want to, they can usually run away, it happens a lot. In England it's hard for them, sure. They'll usually get hit by cars, eventually, or picked up by pest control and put down, or returned home again if they've got a chip. Other places, they'll live as strays. But the dogs don't see that at the time, do they? The important moment for them is when they take the decision to go, to take charge of their freedom and change their unhappy lives. I've treated a lot of dogs who have run away and their owners have no idea why." Nyree passed Tina the joint.

"It's interesting," said Frederica, who was sharing the other joint with Neil.

"Sure, some people can spend years in therapy just learning not to fear their freedom," said Nyree. "You know the biggest regrets of people who are dying? It's having not used their freedom to live true to themselves and to follow their own path. Close after that, it's having worked too hard."

I nodded to myself. I should have guessed it.

"It's not only freedom. People also struggle to deal with other fears they have deep down. Most problems that people have eventually boil down to one of just a few things."

"Like what?" Tina exhaled a cloud of smoke and offered me the joint. I passed, so did Red and Jen. She handed it back to Nyree.

"Death is a big one, maybe the biggest. For people that is, not dogs. Dogs don't think about the future in the same way as us. Fear of death is an interesting one for me. I understand it in individuals, but I want to know why people collectively know that they're killing themselves, by killing the living planet, but carry on doing it anyway. It's like we're *trying* to kill ourselves."

"But don't you know that reefer's killing you, Ny?" pointed out Neil, taking his own joint back from Frederica. He had his shave kit laid out on the ground beside him and had been slowly and meticulously honing and stropping the blade of his olive wood-handled straight razor while listening to the discussion, a manner he had of relaxing sometimes. "If that's your argument, I could say that *you're* trying to kill yourself, but you're just pretending that you're not."

Nyree acknowledged this, nodding. "That's a good point. Thank you, Neil, for that. I'm going to think about that one some more. Yes." She reflected for a few moments. "So, which ones have we done. Freedom and death," she reminded herself. "I suppose *then* there's the meaning of life, or, like, the lack of a meaning of life, I should say. Again, that's no problem for dogs, but it's a big one for some people. No-one here I'm guessing."

Red came to life. "Nah, I worked out that life was pointless when I was about fifteen. But then I found a reason to live..." he went to put his arms around Jen. She smiled and opened her arms in an embrace, but at the last moment he ducked past her and picked up the bottle of whisky next to her on the ground, holding it aloft with both hands.

"Thank you!" he cried emotionally up to the starlit sky, eyes closed.

Nyree watched this display with mild amusement, blowing a gentle stream of smoke from between her pursed lips. "Well done, Red," she said, and moved on to the next of her collection of mortal and canine fears that must be conquered for one to lead a happy life.

"Next, there's being alone. Even here, now, we're all together, yeah, but really we're alone, we're a collection of individuals, each one of us all on our own, just like when we're born and when we die. We just try and alleviate the loneliness with company."

"Huh, it's not working with this crummy company," interjected Red, feigning hurt that nobody had laughed at his whisky joke.

"Same with dogs?" smiled Tina, ignoring Red's comment.

"Right, they're always making new friends!" puffed Nyree, nodding. "Then, maybe the biggest with dogs, quite important for people too, is, kinda like, being *special*. Dogs get sad if they're not looked up to by other dogs, or if they're not up there in the, like, hierarchy. Some people are the same, they can't bear to think that other people don't respect them, or don't admire them, or won't remember them after they die, or whatever. So they wreck their lives, and other people's as well, doing things to try to get other people to like them. A lot of the time they're seeking approval from their parents. They never learn that they're just one more person and that nobody really cares about them or what they do, deep down, not even their parents. That's why you've gotta do things for yourself, and not for other people – call it selfish if you like. It's *good* to be selfish, in that sense."

"Are you afraid to die?" she suddenly asked Tina.

The question caught Tina off-guard. "Um, I don't know. I don't really think about it," she replied.

Nyree looked at her. She was reclined on Joe's supine figure, her face illuminated by the glowing camp fire, the stub of the joint smouldering between her thumb and fingers. Joe was now sleeping beneath the stars.

"You shouldn't be," she said softly.

"I get all of that, Ny," Red spoke again. He was pouring himself another whisky. Nyree looked over at him. "But what I'm not clear on, is the dogs. Can we go back to that...? Why do they sniff each other's behinds, man? That's what *really* scares me."

XXII

We rose late. Red and Jen had slept in the Kombi and I was awoken by the creak of the back door opening as they got out. Jen had found one of the slingshots we had bought in Buenos Aires and was firing stones at cacti when I emerged from our tent, dehydrated and with eyes half-closed and puffed-up. I challenged her to an impromptu target-shooting contest and she summarily destroyed me without even trying. I could barely see straight to aim. She was an excellent shot. "This was how we played as children," she told me.

After all the morning rituals, we got on the road again and made the border town of La Quiaca around noon. We joined the expected long line of traffic and waited, nearing the bridge that crossed over to Villazón in Bolivia a couple of hours later. As we approached a group of policemen and women near the border control office, we were waved over. The four girls, minus Jen, sat up front. This had been our strategy for passing checkpoints until now. With Little Billie's Brazilian licence plate and the complexions of the girls, we hoped they would assume that we were *Brasileiros* returning from Argentina to Brazil to avoid the strife with

157

Chile. It seemed to have worked so far. We had been stopped very few times on the way north, despite the many roadblocks.

Tina wound down the passenger-side window on the right of the van to speak to the officer who lumbered towards us, a tall, overweight man with knock-knees, and they exchanged greetings.

"*Buenos días, Señorita*. We want to speak to you about the killing of an animal last night," he said into the window.

I suddenly went empty inside and missed a breath. *The llama?* It hadn't even occurred to me that the plods could have found out about that. There had been nobody around the previous night and nobody when we had left that morning either. Tina looked over her shoulder at me in the back. As one of the two principal Spanish-speakers, Frederica being the other, I was called on. I quickly tried to straighten myself out as I was dishevelled from the drinking and camping the previous night. My breath reeked. Frederica remained sitting in the driver's seat. I climbed out of the back door, squeezing past Joe and Red, and walked around to where the plod was standing.

"*¿Sí, señor?*" I cordially saluted him.

He repeated what he had initially said. "We want to speak to you about the killing of an animal last night."

I looked at him blankly, assisted in this by my whisky hangover, which was now reaching its peak, and made ten times worse by the three thousand seven hundred metre altitude. Whisky was borderline lethal at these elevations. "Have I understood you correctly, an animal?" I replied, hoping that the plods were still unsure as to who had done it.

WONDERING, THE WAY IS MADE

"Yes, we know you lot did it. A *campesino* reported to us that his llama had been slaughtered by a group of Brazilians last night." He looked at me with a smug, slovenly glint.

My terrible headache and slowed reactions were a huge benefit at this moment, suppressing my instinctive emotional response and anxiety, and helping me to think bluntly. He knew about the llama but I decided that he was bluffing about the Brazilians. "I'm sorry to hear about the killing of the animal, *señor*, but it has nothing to do with us. None of us are Brazilian."

The glint faded in his eye. He fixed me with a stare, then looked at the girls in the front seat, then looked back at me. I could see that he hadn't been making up the thing about the Brazilians. Someone had told him that. He did not seem impressed and said nothing, not even asking for identification. I put myself into his mind and envisioned the desperately dull life of manning this border post, wishing away the endless hours spent breathing dust and exhaust fumes, griping all day with colleagues, dodging paperwork and living off the hope of the sweeteners that came from easy targets and lucky catches.

I spoke to him again. "Perhaps, in the light of what has happened, we could offer a small donation to the community to help compensate for the loss of their animal. We have very much enjoyed this enchanting place and the people have been most kind to us. It would be the least we could do to assist."

From the left breast pocket of my shirt I took the small instruction manual that had come with our satellite internet hub, from which I had removed the cover to leave it looking, at a distance, as though it could feasibly be a piece of official documentation. In the middle of it a twenty dollar note protruded slightly. I passed him the booklet and he flicked through it as though inspecting it, at the same time pocketing the money with a legerdemain befitting a conjuror.

"Hm," he mused, giving me back the booklet, which I put back in its pocket, ready to be reloaded with dollars and used another day.

When the big plod spoke again, it was with the air of one pontificating on universal truths. "These are poor people and the llama are their livelihood. They are very valuable to them. When they are killed, it is serious."

On the other side of the Kombi the traffic continued to pass by us and over the bridge. A haze of dust hung in the air and the midday sun burned intensely through the rarefied atmosphere. The rest of the plods still stood in a group nearby. Looking as natural as possible, I opened the passenger door of the Kombi and went into the glove box in the cabin, resting the lid of it on Tina's knees. I took my wallet from the pocket of my jeans and, pretending to rummage through the glove box, removed a one hundred dollar bill from the wallet and left it resting on the inner lid. I came back out and closed the door, deftly presenting my passport to the plod at the same time in order to make it look like that was what I had been retrieving. It was like a dance. He took my passport, opened it to the photo page, casually looked into the passenger window and spirited the bill into the shirt pocket of his uniform, then handed the passport back to me.

"Bien," he said. "You must get your passports stamped here." He pointed at the office on the bridge. "The Bolivian control is next door."

Leaving the Kombi parked where it was, everyone got out and we got our stamps from both sides, then got back into Little Billie and drove across the bridge and into

Villazón. Nobody talked until we were safely into Bolivia.

Red broke the silence. "Okay, guys, what're we eating tonight? Llama steaks?!" We all laughed hard with relief.

"Pheeeeweeee!" whistled Tina. "Well played, Joss!"

"We were outrageously lucky." My arms and legs had gone weak and were shaking lightly with what felt like a combination of mild post-shock euphoria and delirium tremens. "But how in the hell did they know about the llama? We were in the middle of nowhere!"

"Bush telegraph, mate, must've been. I can't work it out either," said Neil.

Frederica spoke up. "In Italy, it's the same, in the villages in the mountains. The places where they still speak in dialect. Everybody knows everything right away, like magic. It seems as though they know what you are going to do before you do it yourself."

Jen nodded at these words, from which I surmised that things were similar in Mongolia as well.

"It's incredible," was all I could say. I was uncomfortable and wanted to lie down, but with five in the back of Little Billie, the days of being able to do that were now gone.

"It's what they had before closed-circuit television, internet monitoring and the plod state," announced Joe. "Some people are just nosy and have to know everything and gossip about it, it's in their nature. They're more generally known as *women*. They're the 'bush telegraph'." He raised a hand to pre-empt a verbal attack from Tina. "You get some blokes who are gossips as well, I'll concede, Tina. Then, on top of that, you get the people who are paid for being nosy, like that jobsworth back there."

Nyree berated him from the front seat. "We *killed* someone's *llama*, Joe. I said at the time we shouldn't do it. That guy was alright. He didn't have to let us across the border. Why do you have such a problem with authority?"

"He was alright because we gave him a hundred and twenty dollars," Joe retorted. "He didn't care about any *campesino*'s llama. He probably despises them, they're Indians. The people, whose llama we killed, kill llamas for a living. And I don't call it a *problem* with authority, I call it a healthy disrespect."

"Anyway," Joe added, "now that it's all over - we hope - can I be the first to coin the term 'Llamagate'?"

XXIII

We were glad to be out of Argentina. Threats of war from Chile rumbled on but nothing happened. The rest of the world continued its gradual decline into chaos. The high Bolivian *Altiplano*, through which we moved, seemed to have been passed by by the outside world, though, and seemed oblivious to it in turn.

Our sense of urgency to head north diminished slightly with the danger of war behind us, and we rested in the town of Tupiza, nestled among canyons, for a couple of days. Joe and Ny visited the nearby village where Butch Cassidy and the Sundance Kid had made their last stand against Bolivian soldiers, plods and locals. There was nothing there now, Joe said.

Leaving Tupiza, we trundled slowly northward towards La Paz on dire roads of rock and dirt, which gave Little Billie and us, her complement of errant souls, a hammering. Around us, in parched fields, locals were working to bring in the harvest of quinoa, and the flat valley bottoms were dotted with dry sheaves of bright reddish-purple stalks. Neil looked aggrieved at the damage that the Kombi was sustaining and inspected her each evening. We would have to stop for repairs in La Paz, he said.

The second morning we skimmed the edge of the giant salt pan at Uyuni, stopping to look out onto its infinite whiteness. We had to wear sunglasses against the glare and our brains sent us conflicting signals, interpreting the brilliant vastness as ice and telling us we were cold at the same time as we were slowly roasted by the sun in the thin air.

"There are islands in the middle," I pointed at the dark silhouette of a hill sitting on the perfectly flat, white horizon, "made of *coral*." This sunk in for a few moments.

"No way!" said Nyree.

"Way, Ny," I replied, "Isn't it amazing?"

"Vish, it's a mindblower. Shame Little Billie's suffering, otherwise we could have had fun here taking her out," lamented Neil gruffly, walking back to the Kombi.

We followed Neil and climbed back into the van to continue on our way but thirty seconds later were forced to abort by a noxious odour that poisoned the atmosphere inside. We all bundled out again onto the hard salt.

"*Jesus Christ!* My eyes! Red, you bastard, was that you?" I accused him, coughing.

"Sorry, it followed me in," Red owned up.

"What is *wrong* with you?"

"Change in diet, I've gotten used to Korean food. I'm missing my *kimchi*. Anyway, quit complaining. You should be thanking me for being considerate enough to drop it outside, rather than in the van. I can't help if it decides to follow me in."

We groaned and opened all of the doors for ten minutes to allow Little Billie to air. Once everyone bar Red was back in again, we made him wait outside for a further minute before he was allowed to enter, to try and avoid a repeat of our previous misfortune. At the second attempt, when we were sure the air was clear, we were back on our way.

~~~~~

To our relief, and that of our backsides, the dirt road gave way, finally, to a metalled highway that crossed an immense, mountain-bordered plain, littered with small settlements that became more numerous the further north we travelled. Soon the settlements all merged into one and brittle-looking, half-finished, half-broken buildings spread out as far as the eye could see across the plain, all the way to both horizons. Many were painted with slogans and in places there were stuffed mannequins dangling ominously from nooses tied to street lamps and roofs, warnings to would-be thieves. We drove through this landscape for an hour.

"This is El Alto, I've read about it," Joe told us.

Tina expressed surprise. "We're not even at La Paz yet?"

"It kind of is La Paz. It started out as a satellite town, but it's now bigger than La Paz itself," he explained.

"Blow me, man. It's worse than North Korea," said Red. Jen laughed. "But still not as bad as Hull!" he added, knocking Ottawa's sister town over the border in Quebec, then qualified himself, "You have to be Ontarian to find that funny."

Neil, who was driving, stared out of the window. "Look at the construction of these houses. It's *shocking*," he said scornfully. "I've got no time for people who can't take pride in their own houses."

"They're poor people," Nyree defended.

"It makes no difference," went on Neil. "With the same materials you could do a job that's ten times better. One or two are finished up properly. The rest are a *disgrace*. I'd be shot back home if I did a job like that." He pointed through the windscreen towards a typical example. "It's dangerous, for all sorts of reasons. All those gaps and holes in the brickwork will get insects living in them. You can get diseases that way. People'll get breathing problems from the damp as well."

"Hey, I've had chunks of corn in my turds that can build better houses," joked Red, not noticing Nyree, who looked sad.

"Thanks for that valuable contribution, Red," Tina chided him.

"There are different ways to be poor, Ny," Neil carried on. "Where I was working in Africa, in Botswana, the locals were dirt poor, like they are here. But if you'd told any one of them that they had to sit inside, in front of a computer, for eight hours every day to make a living they would have thought you were crazy. It would have been like a prison sentence for them, and it would have ruined their way of life. They would see *that* as being poor, but there are plenty of people back home that live like that. We've got to look for a repair place," he suddenly switched subject, scanning both sides of the road. "There're a million of them, but they all look like they're run by gangsters."

WONDERING, THE WAY IS MADE

Between the buildings, there were numerous yards that advertised tyres, spare parts and auto repairs, the signs often scrawled in paint on corrugated iron gates. Tough men in tracksuits and baseball caps stood in the road outside several of them. "I'll wait until we're properly in La Paz." Just as Neil said this he pulled over to the side of the road.

"Why are you stopping?" Tina asked him.

"We'll give this girl a lift. Pop the back door, Joss," he instructed.

I opened the back door and a young girl of no more than fifteen climbed in. She was dressed in the attire of long skirt, stockings and brightly coloured smock that the majority of women on the *Altiplano* wore, but without the traditional, narrow bowler hat that adorned the heads of many. Her hair was tied back. She carried a baby in a bright pink striped woven blanket on her back, tied at the front. A fresh breeze from outside blew in as she entered.

"*¿Ciudad?*" I asked, closing the door again. She nodded. "She's going to the centre, Neil," I called up, and he pulled out into the traffic again. The girl squeezed on to the end of the bunk opposite me, alongside Tina, sitting on the edge to leave space for her baby, who was remarkably calm and silent. I marvelled at how such healthy-looking individuals could appear from this grim hell-hole on the high mountain plains. I asked her some questions, but she was too shy to talk, or perhaps just didn't want to. I settled back in my seat and returned to looking out of the back window. I tried at these times to always stay attentive, to be receptive to the small glimpses and clues as to the magic of whatever place we were passing through, and to draw as much as I could from the fleeting, ever-changing visions of the world passing by me on the other side of the glass. Even here, behind all the grimness, there had to be magic, this was evident from the mysterious vitality that the quiet girl had brought into the van with her.

Billie limped the last miles into the city of La Paz, down the descent from the plain, through trees and into the steep-sided valley that bounded this astonishing metropolis in the mountains. Saw-toothed ridges, rocky pinnacles and the shining white summits of Illimani and Huayna Potosi stood sentinel over precarious suburbs clinging to the mountainsides and tumbling to the valley floor.

There was no chance of camping in the city. We dropped off the girl and checked into a hotel. Neil and Freddie volunteered to take charge of finding a mechanic for Little Billie, and we laboriously unloaded everything from the back of her into our rooms before they set out.

Tina and I crashed into bed and made love for the first time since we had started north from Santa Rosa. Afterwards, I keeled over like a spent salmon and fell into a catatonic sleep amid the cacophony of the incessant car horns of this insane, raw city.

XXIV

It took four days to get Little Billie fixed up. Neil and Freddie oversaw the work, Neil helping out as a mechanic and Freddie translating. The rest of us did our own things. It was healthy to spend some time apart from each other and there was plenty to see in the city. The narrow, hilly side-streets were teeming with markets of every description, and we lost ourselves for hours in the maze of thronging crowds. There were markets for fish, shoes, televisions, bowler hats, fruit, witchcraft, textiles, live animals, bread, alcohol and meat, and anything else you could think of. They were each confined to a small, defined area of the city, often just a few streets, and were run by syndicates of migrants from the different regions of Bolivia who had settled in those areas, bringing their skills and wares with them from their lands. At night there would be raucous processions and music in the streets, always against the backdrop of blaring car horns.

When we all reconvened at the end of the four days, still tired from the relentless noise and movement of La Paz, we had a new arrival, a black kitten that Nyree had found in distress in a gutter. "Everybody, meet Paz," she introduced her, "I just couldn't leave her, she was helpless."

"Awww! What a fluffball! She's adorable!" Tina tickled her under the chin and the kitten licked her fingers.

"Paz. Like as in *La* Paz?" asked Neil.

"Peace. *Paz* means peace, Neil. It's a nice name," Freddie enlightened him.

"*Peace?* Whoa, that's just too hippy, man." Red looked surprised at our new addition. "How will we take it on the boat?"

"Cats can live on boats. She can catch mice and rats. We will definitely have them," said Frederica knowledgeably.

Joe also tried to assuage Red's concern. "Don't worry, Red, mate. Ny kept the cat on the condition that I was allowed a pet, too. Allow me to introduce you to Pies, *La* Pies." He held up what looked like a small, desiccated llama, about six inches long. "Only cost me twenty Bolivianos," he boasted. "He'll bring us good fortune and protect us against future Llamagates!"

"Oh! We saw them in the witches' market!" exclaimed Jen.

"Uh-huh. They use them as offerings to *Pachamama*, their Mother Earth, to bless land where they're going to build. They bury them under the foundations," explained Joe.

Tina was still in the dark. "But what is it?"

"A llama foetus. They keep the young llamas that are still-born just for that purpose."

"Still-born? What?! That is grim, Joe. *You* are grim!" Tina told him.

Red tickled Pies under the chin, winding Tina up. "Hey, he's cute, man. Look at him, he likes to be tickled! *Goochie goochie goo!*" Joe wiggled Pies, playing along, as Red tickled. "Y'know, Jen and I heard that for big constructions, bridges and skyscrapers and such, where *Pachamama* really needs something good, they'll use *people* instead of these dead llamas. Those people that you see everywhere around here, wasted, passed out in doorways? They go missing all the time, apparently. And, sometimes," he added forebodingly, "*backpackers!*" He tickled Pies again, slowly, and sang with a haunting voice, *"Goochie goochie goo!"*

Tina screwed up her face at him in disdain as we got into the van. Neil insisted on driving again, saying that he wanted to see the difference now that Little Billie had been repaired. Nobody argued. He jumped into the driver's seat, with Freddie and Nyree alongside him up front, Nyree holding Paz on her lap. In the back, Tina sat as far away as she could from Joe and Red, and Pies. A couple of coughs from the engine, a judder, and with a slow heave we, and the freshly laden Little Billie, were back on the road.

~~~~~

"I've been on the web quite a bit," mentioned Joe as we made our way out of the city, passing again through the sprawling, ramshackle plain of El Alto. I looked out of the back window and saw it, this time, in a completely different way. I imagined each decrepit, melancholy building as a gravestone for the tiny, still-born llama that lay beneath. Perhaps Red was right, and people lay beneath some of them. I was looking out onto a vast cemetery. Maybe that was the magic of the place that I had sensed when the quiet girl and her child had climbed into the van. This city, if you could call it that, was inhabited by spirits.

If anything, though, rather than being blessed by *Pachamama*, it felt cursed. I felt sorry for the quiet girl and her small child.

"Have you seen the latest thing out of the UK?" Joe's voice halted my reverie.

"The conscription thing?" I asked. Tina and I had spent a lot of time in internet cafes during the days in La Paz, learning all that we could about maritime navigation and downloading books, nautical and celestial charts, and logarithmic navigation tables. In between, I had brought myself abreast of events in the world.

"What's that?" Neil pricked up his ears. "I've been underneath this van the last four days, I'm out of the loop."

Joe spoke. "Yeah, they reckon they want to conscript everyone to help defend against mass civil breakdown. They're doing it in waves. It's a ridiculous idea in the first place, but, get this, if you fail to respond, you're liable to *prosecution*."

"I've never agreed with prostitution," said Red in a sombre voice.

"Yeah, right! Red!" giggled Jen. "Everybody know why you came to Korea!"

"But what if we're abroad?" Neil was vexed at Joe's news.

"Right, you've got two weeks to respond when they send it out. After that, they can press charges. You can appeal apparently, so I guess that would cover people that are out of the country," Joe expanded.

Neil, from the driver's seat, looked over his shoulder

in disbelief before looking back at the road. "Why don't they think these things through?"

"It's simple," explained Joe. "It's like I was saying the other day – make everyone a criminal and then you can arrest and persecute whoever you want. The only way out this time is to sign up, but then they've got you by the balls anyway, it's just as bad."

Neil shook his head. "I want to say it can't work, but the problem is that it probably will. What complete bastards. Well, that does it. If I wasn't sure before, I am now. I'm not going back until there's a new system. Sod it, England's not that good." He put his hand on Freddie's knee, alongside him, and looked at her entreatingly. "Freddie, *amore mio*, how do you fancy New Zealand?"

"Neil! Look at the road!" she laughed.

"That's actually what we're thinking, longer term," said Nyree, still stroking Paz, who was asleep.

"Yeah, but hold on, to get the New Zealand passport I'd have to *marry* you, wouldn't I? I need more time. I'm going to have to think about it some more!" Joe projected to the front.

"Somebody slap him back there!" Nyree shouted back jovially.

Joe chuckled and changed the subject. "The other thing, I found a guy selling a boat in Lima. It looks good to me, but you and Neil'll have to look at it, Freddie. I emailed him. He told me to get in touch with him when we arrive there, and he can meet us in a marina in a place called Barranco. It's in the city."

"Cool, mate, that's a good start. Show us the pictures when we stop," enthused Neil.

"Awesome, Joe," I agreed. "What was that bloke like that you worked with on the Kombi, by the way, Neil?" I asked him.

"About yea big, slopey shoulders, bit of a belly," Neil replied succinctly, as though that was the information I had requested. He held out a flat hand to indicate the man's height relative to him. He was being sincere.

"To talk to, you biffer."

"Oh. It went like this. I'd say *'llave!'* and he'd pass me a spanner. Then I'd say *'martillo!'* and he'd pass me a hammer. Freddie taught me those words. *'Llave! Martillo!'* That was about it. Alright sort of bloke. Freddie chatted to him a bit and I just worked. Little Billie's running like a dream now, though."

~~~~~

We cruised for hours and reached our next objective, the shores of the mighty Lake Titicaca. Further along the lake we would have our final border crossing the next day, into Peru. There was little traffic when we reached the water. We queued and drove the Kombi onto one of the rickety floating vehicle platforms that plied the Tiquina straits, where the lake narrows to a small channel. We crossed on a separate passenger boat and watched from the opposite bank, with our hearts in our mouths, as Little Billie and all of our worldly possessions crossed the rough waters of the straits on the half-rotten, patched-up raft that twisted visibly as it rode the waves. We hadn't realised the extent of its decrepitude when we had driven onto it and now expected to see it go down at any moment. When the hard-faced, tracksuited yokel that piloted the raft brought it in safely, we were too uptight to thank him.

"Won't someone point out the bloody obvious to

him, and tell him that if he doesn't get that raft fixed up pronto, he's going to be blowing bubbles? I don't mind if he wants to kill himself, but I'd have been upset if he'd sunk Little Billie," commented Neil. The pilot suspected that he was being talked about and fixed him with a murderous look. We were glad to get away.

We drove some more and then decided to camp for the night on the dry, brown, hilly and sparsely populated spit of land that jutted into the water at Yampaputa. Joe wanted to see an island near there, and it was only a short detour from the road that led to the Peruvian border. We got to the end of the peninsula in the late afternoon.

"There it is," said Neil, pulling up on the headland. "Is that it?"

We could see the island, a bare, brown protrusion from the ocean-like lake. Around it, the late afternoon wind whipped the water's surface into white horses. It was odd to think that we stood nearly four thousand metres above the sea, when it seemed we were looking out into it.

Joe had been reading about the island. "It's called the *Isla del Sol*. The Island of the Sun. I just wanted to see it. There's a submerged city built of stone, in the lake just on the other side of the island, behind those hills. They discovered it not all that long ago. It's six thousand years old, with a huge temple. They don't even know who built it," he said to nobody in particular. "And then, on the island itself, there's a place that was sacred for the Inca. More or less like their Stonehenge, but with a labyrinth."

There it was, magic.

"You should go there, Joe," said Nyree. She clutched Paz, who was pawing at her grey llama wool jumper, to her chest.

"Nah, I think it would be like that Butch Cassidy place. They've pulled all the trees down, fished the lake empty, wiped out the giant frogs that used to live here, and now they live off tourists. I just wanted to see it from here."

The death of magic, I thought to myself.

Joe looked out at the island. I could see him trying to imagine what it had been like, first when the mysterious city of stone had been at its height, then later, when it was swallowed by the waters of the lake and the Inca had risen to power.

"They used to sacrifice people here. The prettiest girls, mostly," Joe said, pausing to contemplate. "Can you imagine? I bet they were all fighting each other, throwing themselves onto the altar, begging to be sacrificed, just to reassure themselves that they were the most beautiful."

Tina groaned. "Urgh, not again, Joe! You're so *stupid!*"

"If that's what you think, Tina, here's a *quiz du philosophe*," Joe baited her. "Would you rather be beautiful, but we have to sacrifice you, or ugly, with a big hunchback, no neck, cross-eyed and covered in carbuncles, but you don't have to be sacrificed?"

"That's a stupid question."

"It's not supposed to be an easy question. It's a *quiz du philosophe*."

When Joe said *quiz du philosophe*, he sang it in a low, theatrical voice. We played this game when we wanted to present a difficult choice, or a conundrum, to each other. The secret was in identifying something that was very close to someone's heart, a weakness, and the comedy was in seeing how far they would debauch themselves to avoid losing it.

"I'd rather live, that's obvious," said Tina.

"Is it? I don't believe you..." Joe teased. "Go on, you have to say it... '*I would rather be covered in carbuncles*', and mean it."

Tina took a swipe at him and he dodged, laughing. "That was a bit rough! You know I'm just kidding you," he said.

Red suddenly piped up. "Hey, is that why they're all so funny-looking? They selected out all the good-looking people by sacrificing them?" He was clearly pleased with himself and his lateral thinking.

"That's racist, Redface," said Tina.

"So's calling me Redface," he retorted. "OK, OK. Is that why they *were* all so funny-looking?" he compromised, "And still are?!" he threw back in.

Tina was riled. "No, Redface. It's because your ancestors personally came over and introduced the ugly gene. Along with syphilis and smallpox."

"And homosexuality!" chirped Jen. Her understanding of Anglo-Saxon humour was that homophobic accusations against Red were considered hilarious, and she would frequently introduce them at the most inappropriate times. The joke had evolved beyond its origins to become purely her timing and, of course, the repetition. As it became funnier each time, she would take it as a sign that it was still working, which would reinforce the cycle, and so on – a classic positive feedback loop. At this precise moment her timing was so impeccable, her upbeat expression so perfect and Red so crestfallen, that it was utterly priceless. Everyone but Red collapsed to their knees with unstoppable laughter, even Tina instantly forgetting her crankiness and doubling over in fits of giggles.

Red stood there alone on the desolate headland, silhouetted against the sky and buffeted by the wind, contemplating his spectacular backfire. "Alright!" he conceded, "That went down like a lead turd. You all got me, you goddam' bunch of *Incas*."

~~~~~

Quiz du philosophe – Would you rather remain in the warm, comforting embrace of a world, and a *programme*, that is collapsing around you, and die with it? Or would you leave it and become a lonely free man, out in the cold, for a chance to live?

XXV

The border crossing into Peru the next morning went without incident. Nyree had been worried that they wouldn't let Paz through, but nobody even checked inside the van. Once over the border, we changed some money into Peruvian *soles*, then skirted the western shore of the giant lake, passing through numerous towns and villages that all looked like spin-offs of El Alto.

"This place is just Bolivia with different hats," observed Red. The narrow, darkly coloured bowler hats, worn by the Bolivian women, had been replaced with cloth caps, or stiff hats with long, upturned rims, like bowls, all in vivid colours.

"They're beautiful, aren't they?" said Nyree. "The colours!"

"Hmmm," hesitated Joe. "I don't want to spoil it for you, Ny, but the people are the same here as everywhere else. It's all a big attempt at one-upmanship. The Spanish brought in these clothes when they were here. The *mestizo* Spanish-Indians would wear them to identify themselves as middle class and not to be mistaken for pure-blood Indians. If you want to be harsh, it's a betrayal of their roots."

Nyree frowned. "Why did you tell me that?" she asked.

"Because it's the truth."

Nyree thought on this. "But it's not like that's what they're thinking every morning when they get dressed."

"Hm, maybe not," Joe conceded, "but that's half the reason I could never get a normal job. When I pulled a suit and tie on in the morning I felt as though I was leaving all my principles at home. I was suddenly part of some corporate tribe. It wouldn't have been as bad if I'd been able to wear jeans and a t-shirt. I'd contest that any kind of uniform betrays something of your inner thoughts. You're basically identifying yourself as part of a group. People don't wear them unless it sits right with them. Look at the guys here, they're much less traditional. They're all just wearing tracksuits and trainers."

"Huh, well, I still like the colours, even though the radioactive pink burns my eyes a bit," Nyree said to herself.

~~~~~

It was a further three days before we hit the coast. We first descended from the *Altiplano* into high mountain valleys, where maize was grown in terraced fields, walled with stones, on the steep mountainsides. We passed formidable ruins and stopped in ancient, grey Inca towns built of solid stone. Cacti grew on the thick walls and the tiled roofs of the houses. Red bundles of rags and plastic on wooden poles outside front doors advertised fresh brews of *chicha*. We drank this sour maize brew from great cauldrons in cellars like medieval drinking halls, amongst locals whose faces told the stories of these valleys.

As we dropped out of the mountains, we travelled precarious roads that clung to sheer, rocky slopes. Our appreciation of the majesty of the scenery was tempered by teeth-clenching apprehension at the precipitous death-drops that lay at every bend. Even here, tailgating was common, which did nothing to help the situation. Coca-chewing Peruvian truck drivers careered along these routes with wild abandon, and we would pull over to let them pass whenever we could. Driving these stretches would leave your nerves in tatters. You could not allow your attention to falter for the slightest moment. Following further one-finger driving exploits, Neil had been barred from driving on these steep mountain sections by the girls, so a lot of the driving fell to me.

Eventually, we emerged into the Andean foothills and then into an arid coastal desert of cream-coloured sand and rock. We drove through this empty wilderness for a day before we reached the sea at Pisco. This was our first glimpse of the Pacific Ocean, the ocean that we planned to make our home for the next months and maybe beyond.

We had a ceremonial swim in the Pacific near Pisco's abandoned industrial pier, now in ruins and home to a flotilla of pelicans, boobies and gulls. As we swam, boobies ripped into the water around us in waves like *kamikaze*. Jen did not swim but paddled close to the shore with Red.

Tina swam up alongside me. "First salt water since the Ilha do Mel. I miss that place so much! It feels good, doesn't it?"

"Good and cold," I said. "It would be nice if it was as warm as it was in the Ilha do Mel. I got back into the regular washing thing in La Paz, I've been crying out for a bath since we left!"

"Well, yes, you are smelly!" laughed Tina. "Have you seen the dolphins?"

"Yeah, I heard you shout earlier. They're a different kind from the ones we saw in Brazil, much bigger and darker, False Killer Whales, maybe. What about the pelicans?"

"I know!" she exclaimed. "It's the first time I've ever seen one. The dolphins look so happy. They're just having fun!"

My teeth were starting to chatter from the cold water, even though it was a warm day. "Right, I'm getting out before my balls retract any further. They're already up around my Adam's apple like a bow-tie and my teeth are chattering. How are you not cold?"

"I am, a bit. It must be time for some lunch, anyway," said Tina, treading water. Before we started swimming back to the beach, she added, "I'm happy now, Joss. I've thought a lot about what Ny said on the night we spent around the fire, when you killed that llama – but we won't talk about Llamagate! I think the problem before we met all the others, and that night... it was that I was afraid. It was making me unhappy. Maybe I *was* afraid to die, like Ny said, at the root of it – I don't know. I've stopped being a scaredy-cat. I like what we're doing now. You don't have to worry – we don't need to have that talk any more... I've straightened things out in my mind. I'll show you my diary – it's been interesting these last few weeks!"

With these words from Tina, a huge weight was lifted from me. I felt that I would float right up and out of the water. We had not yet followed up from our talk of the night I had killed the llama, and it had been hanging over us. Tina's dark eyes looked at me across the glistening, green water. She had tied her afro back in a bun in an attempt to keep it from getting wet, but it shone with droplets of sea water. The contrast of her brightly patterned swimsuit against her brown skin, and the water, was beautiful.

"Cool, T, you have no idea how relieved I am to hear you say that. If you weren't happy, I wouldn't be either," I said. "I love you."

I blew a kiss as best as I could across the wavelets and she caught it and blew one back. It was true, I did love her. I knew that I was doing the right thing when she shone with happiness. If she grew sad, I knew that I was going wrong somewhere, even if I could not fathom where. We raced back to the shore to warm ourselves up.

~~~~~

The city of Pisco had been shattered by an earthquake years before. The quaint, colonial city that had stood there for centuries vanished in an instant, and in its place were now hastily erected edifices of brick and concrete, *a la* El Alto. The seafront remained abandoned and in ruins, and was being reclaimed by nature. Across the shimmering bay, in the distance, the desert peninsula of Paracas was visible, protruding from the sea like a lump of bone. Some of the large, black dolphins that we had seen earlier were playing in the bay over in that direction. The boobies still took turns to tear into the water, hunting fish. Looking up and down the endless, empty beach, I wondered if this snapshot of the decimated Pisco was a foretaste of things to come for other parts of the world. It wasn't so bad, I thought.

After swimming, we pulled Little Billie up on a stretch of the promenade by an abandoned basketball court and ate lunch facing the sea. The air here was different from that in the mountains, fuller and thicker, and with the faintest taste of salt. It felt as though it poured into our lungs when we breathed in. Our lunch was flatbread, cured sausage, raw onions and fruit juice.

Red watched the diving birds as he ate. "The sea is just *great*, man. I love the sea. It always has the best animals."

Nyree eyed him suspiciously, surprised at the absence of sarcasm in Red's comment. "That's because it's the only place left that hasn't been, like, totally destroyed by people. Even though we're doing a pretty good job. I mean, I find this hard to get my head around, but before crude oil everything was run on *whale oil*. Can you imagine topping up the Kombi there with whale oil?" She fed a morsel of sausage to Paz, who played around her feet.

"Yeah," said Neil casually, and then, "What?!" as Nyree shot him a withering look.

She went back to Red's sea animals. "There used to be a beautiful, giant sea-cow that used to walk around near the shore, using its front fins as legs to graze on sea grasses in the shallows. It was tame and never dived underwater. Once they were discovered by sailors, they were all gone within thirty years."

"Did not know that," I said, nodding my acknowledgement of this good knowledge. "It's sad, Ny, but there are a lot of things like that. The Moa birds in New Zealand all got wiped out by people, many species, you'll know about that. And the giant eagles that used to hunt the Moa. Same for all the giant lemurs in Madagascar. Even the tiger has nearly gone now. The planet we have now is barren and sterile compared to how it was before. What we see are just the faint echoes of all the abundant life there used to be. The vitality is gone. What eats me is that we think what we see is as good as it gets, because we don't know any better. We're like kids who've been given a beaten-up, blown-out, plastic football but still think it's the best thing ever because we've never seen a proper one."

"Generational amnesia," murmured Joe.

I realised from everyone's faces that I'd digressed onto something that was too heavy for the present discussion. There was no sense in getting yourself down about these things. By definition, you just ended up feeling down. Therein lay the paradox. Our foolish collective optimism allowed us to overlook the tragedies we had perpetrated against ourselves as the price for continuing to feel good about ourselves. Optimism ruled the day, keeping us sane, while smilingly sidestepping its part of the blame. Like Epictetus, we did not worry about those things that we could not change. I switched tack: "It's not about the sea, technically, but did you know that in Lake Nicaragua there are freshwater sharks? It used to be part of the ocean, but since it broke away, the sharks that were trapped there adapted to live in fresh water."

"That's vish," approved Neil, who then contributed a sea story of his own. "I was speaking to some guy who told me about this cave, underwater, in the Solomon Islands. He'd been there. You swim into it and there are all these flashing urchins on the walls that illuminate the place, it's dark. They all pulse at the same time, like strobe lights. He said it blew him away – it was like being at a silent, underwater rave."

"Whoa!" enthused Red. "*Anything* that glows is just too cool. Like those jack-o'-lantern mushrooms. *Glow-in-the-dark mushrooms, man!* I've always wanted to see those."

"I thought we were talking about sea creatures?" said

Nyree to him with a frown, her hope of engaging in sincere conversation with Red giving way to mild despair.

"There is too much to see!" Freddie injected a positive note, sighing and smiling. "But we can try!"

~~~~~

After a group vote, it was agreed that we would spend the afternoon looking for boats in the small nearby fishing and tourist town of Paracas. Pisco, despite its size, did not appear to have a harbour. We drove fifteen minutes down the coast in the direction of the peninsula until we saw a small harbour. We pulled up and got out amidst a cluster of moto-taxis, leaving Red and Jen to look after the Kombi. There was a lot of activity around a fish market by the harbour entrance. Pelicans clustered on the roof of the market and waddled defiantly around the pungent-smelling yard with their long bills pulled close against their breasts, scavenging for scraps. We made our way through the market to the harbour beyond, our brightly painted Kombi, ragged appearance and the presence of the girls drawing looks.

"No sailboats. Only motor-powered. No good for us," surmised Neil, looking out onto the water, within seconds of arriving. "I was hoping for more, to be honest."

"It's true," agreed Frederica.

Ranks of similar-looking fishing vessels in gaudy colours rocked gently alongside each other in the harbour, loaded with fishing gear and with complements of pelicans and gulls. We had been followed to the water's edge by a motley band of stray dogs, including two of the Peruvian hairless variety. These dogs had been bred in these lands since before the Inca. Their lean build, smooth, black skin and long ears recalled those ancient Egyptian dog statues that were used to guard tombs. It was as though a pair of them had suddenly awakened, climbed down from their plinths and joined us in the hunt for a sailing vessel. As we stood looking out onto the boats, the dogs lined up on the edge of the dock, inquisitively scanning the water too.

"Why are these dogs taking such an interest in us?" said Joe suspiciously. Then, as though he had had a revelation:

"My *god*. You've *synchronised!*"

He said this in an accusatory tone, as though unmasking a voodoo practitioner. I didn't get his meaning straight away but I saw Tina flush slightly and then I understood. His perception was uncanny and now I thought about it, the dogs were taking an unusual interest in us. Tina's lady days were on the way, a time of the month that I referred to as "Hurricane Tina" as she was prone to outbursts of crankiness.

"Hurricane Tina is on the way," I said, cryptically. I received a light slap on the arm from Tina, who was unamused by the expression, and a number of baffled looks from the others.

"A hurricane?" queried Frederica.

"Hurricane *Tina*," I said quietly, motioning towards Tina with my head and hoping to avoid another slap, then laughed. It clicked amongst the others, along with Joe's meaning, and there were smiles. The dogs sensed that they were involved and looked at us hopefully, tails wagging.

Neil walked over and crouched among them. They crowded around him, all eager to investigate. He seemed to be able to commune with them.

Nyree watched him with a smile. "They like you, Neil. You've got a way with them," she said. "You can stand in for some of my Reiki sessions, if you like. Are you part dog or something?"

"Yeah - the ass," interjected Joe, to some collective amusement.

We didn't waste our time looking any further in this place. Asking in the market, I learned of another small harbour further down the bay. We drove there, on the way Joe harking back to the dogs and telling us stories. He told us that in some parts of the world, before firearms became widespread and when villages were still terrorised by wild beasts, menstruating women would be bundled together into a single hut for the duration of these days. In small communities, they would generally be synchronised in their cycles, so they would all go through this together.

"Feminists will tell you that it was because the men were barbaric and uneducated, and thought the spontaneous shedding of blood was a form of witchcraft. In fact, it was the most common-sense and efficient way to ensure that they were safe and could be *protected*, as animals from miles around would come at night to investigate. If you're fighting off lions with spears, it's best to have all your womenfolk in one place."

"You see, T?" I whispered in her ear, "The things I get you to do are for your own good."

"If you know what's good for you, you'll shut your trap right now," she hissed back.

"Don't get cranky, my louve."

"I'm *not* cranky."

"OK, Cranks," I teased, and suffered a pinch on the

leg. Hurricane Tina had made landfall.

At the next harbour, the story was the same as for the first. There were many fishing boats and many of them were for sale, harbour-bound by high fuel prices. However, none of them were built for sails. After all the anticipation of beginning the search for our boat, it was a disappointment to see not even one that would have served us, as well as a worry. Our hopes would now have to rest on Lima.

XXVI

We left Pisco at first light to get some miles in before breakfast. We were beginning to weary of being constantly on the move and hoped that, with our arrival in Lima, this would be our last day on the road. Joe was at the wheel, his country music playing. Pies the llama foetus dangled on a string from the stub of the rear-view mirror and swung from side to side as we drove, alongside Nyree's string of beads. Joe was only allowed this arrangement when he was driving, "for good fortune". The rest of the time, Pies lived in his pocket.

Leaving the city, we passed extensive fishmeal factories and a series of unimaginably grim, prison-like, walled industrial installations topped with razor wire, before reaching the hollow expanse of the desert. There were infrequent oases where vineyards grew in scruffy desert towns along the coastal highway. Other than that, occasional, remote mines out amid the rock and sand were the only signs of life.

"Reminds me of the Skeleton Coast," reminisced Neil. "When I was guiding in Botswana, we had a month's leave and took Hiluxes out to Namibia, up the coast, and then back into Bots. One Hilux each, just for a laugh. We were always racing. We'd absolutely *hammer* them along these long, open desert roads, sometimes at night, sometimes with the headlights turned out, when we were steaming drunk, stoned, everything. It was an insane trip. One of the guys, Frankie, on the way back, rolled his jeep off the corner of a road and down a ravine, he died. Early on, I remember having to kill this hyena I'd run over at night. I did it with the car jack. A brown hyena, very rare. That still eats me up inside. But all the way up the coast of Namibia it was desert, like this. I could never work out how you got a desert next to the ocean."

"It's the cold current," I said, I was beginning to learn of such things from the study that Tina and I had done so far of marine navigation. "Did you feel how cold it was when we were swimming? The water comes up from the Antarctic with the Humboldt current. It's so cold that barely any of it evaporates, so the air that comes in off the ocean is dry and the coast gets no rain. It'd be my guess that the same thing happens there on the Skeleton Coast. When we get our boat, the Humboldt will be our ride, it'll take us north for a bit, before we reach the currents and winds that'll take us out west."

~~~~~

After three hours or so of driving through desert, a road sign informed us that we were entering a zone of fog. Sure enough, the fog materialised almost immediately.

Nyree was in the front again, in the middle seat with Paz, who by now had become inseparable from her. "Did you see that sign back there? How creepy! How did they know that the fog would be here to put the sign there?"

"It's the *garua*," answered Joe from the driver's seat.

"Herman Melville wrote about it. It hangs over Lima for six months of the year without budging. It does amuse me that it has its own road sign, though. Hopefully it means we're getting near the city."

From where I was sitting, in the front seat by the passenger window, next to Nyree, I could see eerie, seemingly inverted hillsides through the flat, white haze, their bottom slopes bone-yellow and barren, the tops carrying a stubble of plants that eked an existence from what little moisture they could wring from the fog. Later, dwellings began to appear in the desert, rudimentary boxes built far apart from each other and stretching away into the nothingness.

"It's worse than El Alto, man! And that was worse than North Korea!" cried Red in disbelief. "Where have we come to?!"

In the pits of our stomachs we were yearning to get to a place that would allow us to organise our affairs, buy a boat and sail away without undue ceremony and complication, and we were apprehensive to see whether Lima would permit us this favour. Nobody wanted a return to the drawing board, as had happened in Argentina. The hours that followed, driving through the miserable shanties and sprawl of suburban Lima, did nothing to quell our apprehension. We pulled over on several occasions to check our directions, but our maps were next to useless in the chaos of heavy traffic, road works and unmarked streets. There passed what seemed an eternity of frustration, swearing, U-turns and near misses with pedestrians, animals and other vehicles. Then fortune brought us to a spine road with the district of Barranco, our destination, and where we were to meet the boat seller, signposted. Moving at a good pace once we had joined this modern highway, we passed tall, concrete office and residential blocks that gradually gave way to colourful old buildings, trees and small plazas as we branched left, down a hill, and reached the end of the main road at Barranco's central plaza. Numerous vintage cars in fine condition dotted the roadsides of this neighbourhood. Our tension slowly gave way to relief. There was something impalpable about this place that put us at ease.

We parked Little Billie on the plaza and all tumbled out to stretch our stiffened limbs. This was it, the end of our land voyage, and it felt good. Neil and Freddie went off to find us all a place to stay. The rest of us sat in a cafe and ordered drinks. Joe wasted no time and succeeded in getting through on his phone to Rodolfo, the boat owner, who spoke English. We arranged to meet him the next morning.

This part of Lima was perched on high cliffs overlooking a large bay, the Bay of Lima. When Neil and Freddie were back, we walked the short distance to the cliffs that overlooked the sea. The flat, white light of the *garua* fog gave everything a matte appearance and a heaviness, even the water. Already I found myself wishing to see the sky again. To our left, the cliffs became lower and gave way to an isthmus connecting the mainland to a peninsula with a rocky hill on it that delimited the southern sweep of the bay. To our right, the cliffs curved around slowly to where the skyscrapers of the upmarket *Miraflores* district resided atop them. From that stretch of coast, paragliders floated off the cliff tops in the up-draught of the afternoon *vientos alisios*, the trade winds that blew up the coast. We could feel it on the edge where we stood, rising up and over our faces. Out above the bay, a Peruvian military helicopter dropped parachutists into the water, where they were collected by inflatable speedboats. Tina spotted a marina below us, with rows of neatly moored sailboats sitting idle. A shiver ran down my spine. It didn't seem real that we had finally found them. One of them would become ours, something in my innards told me at that moment.

"Joe?" I took a small pair of binoculars from my pocket and passed them to him. "Is it any of those that we were looking at?"

He scanned the marina with the binoculars, resting his elbows on the wall at the cliff edge as he did so, the compass tattooed on his bicep emerging from beneath the sleeve of his t-shirt. He nodded. "It's the brown one. Gitana."

"*Hee-TA-na*. 'Gipsy'," I corrected his pronunciation.

"Right. There's no need to be insulting," he chuckled, passing the glasses back to me. I took them and inspected the *Gitana* as well as I could. I couldn't put my finger on it, but she looked *right*. I experienced a rising sense of excitement in my belly. I was more stoked than I had been at any time on the trip until now. I tried to keep a lid on it. The others took turns to examine her.

"Hey, there's no way I'm getting in *that* heap o' junk, man!" cried Red, causing us all to turn. "Just kiddin'," he cracked, passing to Jen and directing her where to look.

"Fibreglass hull," observed Neil when it came to his turn. He took the glasses from his eyes. "Harder to repair than wood, but I don't see any wooden hulls anywhere, other than the fishing boats further down the bay there, in the open water, but they're all motorised," he said, pointing. He took a second look at the *Gitana*. "It's got a wooden deck and cabin, though. They look in good nick, too. Let's hope it's just as good up close."

"You should be ready for a lot of work with the wood, Neil. We are in the tropics. The rot will invade us if we are not careful," said Freddie in her musical Italian tones.

"I'm ready, *Capitana*. I didn't bring all those tools for nothing." He gave her a kiss on the forehead.

I looked out at the ocean and to the horizon and imagined the eight of us disappearing across it in the tiny vessel floating in the marina beneath us. I looked to my right, across the bay, to the skyscrapers of the city. I felt nothing for it. I looked back at the ocean. Its presence exerted a magnetic pull and mesmerised me. We stood for many minutes gazing out into it like watch-keepers.

XXVII

We met Rodolfo, the boat owner, the next morning at the entrance building of the marina. He arrived promptly at eight o'clock, dressed in an off-white, comfortable suit and open shirt. There was a certain style about him. He had the aura of a man who knew himself, enjoyed life and was comfortable in his own skin. He was in his fifties, tanned and robust, with a moustache, bald head and a firm gaze. He was, we learned, a retired businessman who had operated in the hotel sector. With the recent events around the world, his investments had suffered and he was liquidating some of his assets to buy a new boat for himself and his wife, smaller than the *Gitana*, now that their sons and daughters had grown up. Sailing it would be their retirement project.

He walked us along the pontoon to where the *Gitana* was kept and led us onto the deck at the stern of the vessel, unlocking the cabin. "A drink?" he offered, and we accepted. He descended into the cabin and came back out with a bottle of *pisco*, the Peruvian liquor that shares its name with the shattered city we had come from the previous day, and nine spirit glasses. He poured each of us a measure. "It is to be drunk as follows. First, take a deep breath and hold it. Then, work the *pisco* around the palate." This he did for some seconds, before swallowing and exhaling. "After swallowing, breathe out. This way you will not burn your throat." He poured himself another measure. "*¡Salud!*" he raised his glass.

Standing in a semicircle on the deck, we chinked glasses and drank as he had demonstrated. It worked, the *pisco* descending warmly, but not harshly. Rodolfo poured us another round. "These are for sipping," he said, and indicated for us to be seated on the wooden taffrail that surrounded the stern of the boat, which we did. He deliberated over something he was thinking.

"You are not sailors, are you, except you?" he motioned to Frederica, uncannily. I guessed that he had observed the way she had looked over the boat when she boarded, in a way that none other of us had done.

She seemed to take to him straight away, seeing something in him that the others of us missed, and spoke to him candidly of our voyage, aided, no doubt, by the *pisco*. "Yes. I have sailed with my father in the Mediterranean and the Caribbean. Our idea is to take a boat to New Zealand, for fun, nothing more. We will learn what we need to learn before we go. In our home countries there is trouble now, it is better to spend some time on the ocean, we think." Frederica distilled her words into prismatic sentences of beautiful clarity.

"Hm," Rodolfo nodded, and looked each of us in the eye in turn. "It is no small trip. I took this boat to the Galapagos Islands, one devil of a journey. And to Alexander Selkirk Island, home of your Robinson Crusoe!"

"Did you know that Robert Louis Stevenson spent his final years sailing the Pacific, as well?" said Joe, apropos of Rodolfo's reference.

I corrected his mistake. "That's true, Joe. But you're thinking of *Treasure Island*, I think. *Robinson Crusoe* was Daniel Defoe's."

"Do you know what you're doing?" Rodolfo asked us, kindly. I could see that he was concerned for us. We had not expected this, thinking that the meeting would be a simple negotiation on the price of the boat. Our initial braggadocio had evaporated and we sat there, exposed as greenhorns.

Tina saw that there was no use in bluffing. "In all honesty, no. Not me, anyway. We've read a lot about sailing, given that we knew we were going to do this, but we haven't actually done any, other than Freddie and Nyree. If there's some way you know that we could learn, that'd be amazing."

I saw Rodolfo's genius in offering us the *pisco* truth-elixir when we had arrived. It felt uncomfortable to be making this plea to a man we had just met, but what Tina had said was the truth, there was no arguing.

Rodolfo's eyes gleamed. "You want to start learning now?" He smiled and showed a set of sparkling teeth. "You can see if you like my boat, and she will see if she likes you!" he threw down the gauntlet. He must have liked us.

"Let's get it on!" exclaimed Tina, looking around at all of us, exhilarated. We all rose to our feet.

"One moment please." Rodolfo descended into the cabin once more and returned with a captain's hat. "Now," he began, placing the hat on Frederica's head. It was a touch too big. She pulled a black fabric headband from her jeans pocket and put in on underneath the cap, which now sat perfectly. "You are *la capitana*!" Rodolfo pronounced. "And the best way to learn to captain is to be a captain! Now! You are going to do everything, and I am going to watch. When you have a question, you are going to ask me. Our objective is to sail around the white rocks in the bay that you see there." He pointed out into the bay. "The white colour is *guano*. The island behind the white rocks is *El Frontón*. We will turn around before that, and we will come back. The wind is good this morning. Not too strong. It will be stronger later. OK... now to you." He sat down and poured himself another *pisco*. We all looked at Freddie.

~~~~~

Whether Rodolfo really intended for us to sail that morning, or whether he was testing Freddie, I'm not certain. In any case, for the next two hours Freddie had us performing checks on the boat. Questioning Rodolfo frequently, she gave us a thorough explanation of both the boat itself and of the equipment on board. Neil ran the engine and gave it an inspection. We learned the names of the ropes, the sails, and every other part of the vessel, in a combination of Frederica's poetic voice and Rodolfo's impeccable English. We took notes and listened avidly.

We did not leave the marina that day. Freddie decided that we would pass the afternoon aboard to review what we had learned. Following the thorough examination of the boat, she and Neil had decided that it was for us, and by lunchtime the deal was done. Rodolfo seemed satisfied. We agreed to buy the *Gitana* at the price that had been advertised. We would raise most of the money from the sale of Little Billie. Rodolfo, a consummate businessman, suggested that he take the Kombi in part-payment to streamline the operation and save us bother.

We led him outside, into the car park at the marina

entrance, to see Little Billie, opening the doors so that he could see inside. He looked over her carefully. "Have you noticed all of the beautiful old automobiles in this neighbourhood? It is a kind of fashion for people in the area to keep them. A unique vehicle such as this one will be a great pride for somebody." He agreed that he would take her as he saw her.

We went back to the *Gitana*, and Rodolfo handed us the proof of ownership and maintenance history documents for the boat, along with the keys, which were attached to an empty squeezable lemon to allow them to float if they were dropped in the water. We paid him in cash what we owed him above the value of Little Billie and agreed that we would give him the keys to the Kombi the next morning, once we had unloaded all of her cargo onto the boat and given her a clean. He would then take us on the outing around the white rocks in the bay – our first sailing lesson as a team.

"Under this fine captain, I think you are going to be OK," Rodolfo said, patting Frederica on the shoulder, "but please, be very careful and make many short trips before you leave. I had the same idea with my wife for our new boat, for our retirement together, to simply sail the world. It is very appealing. Perhaps we will go. Perhaps we will be pushed to go, like you have been yourselves. We will see what happens here, in my Peru. She is an incredible country. Do you know? We can produce almost anything we want. We have nearly every type of climate and landscape there is, all within our borders. She will look after herself, I think. But who knows? The world is changing. Friends, I will see you in the morning." He left with a smile and a wave.

XXVIII

That afternoon, we split into our teams. Tina and I, the navigation team, took the tiny cabin in the bow of the boat for a siesta. There were two other double cabins at the stern, alongside each other, and a bunk either side of the main cabin, which also had a small kitchen and water closet. My head spun from trying to take in all of the information from that morning. We decided that we were going to spend the afternoon practising the operation of the on-board navigation systems and transferring all of the electronic navigational charts we had onto them. Rodolfo had suggested that we try to obtain paper charts as a fall-back and had given us the name and address of a bookshop in Lima that we could visit for this purpose.

Tina climbed into the wedge-shaped bed that occupied the entire front cabin and settled next to me. "How lucky were we to meet Rodolfo and find this boat?" she said.

I looked at her with relief. "I know, fortune seems to be smiling on us this time. It almost seems too easy. After finding nothing in Pisco, I was worried there'd be nothing here either. I had visions that we'd have to steal onto a boat in the dead of night and sail it away like pirates. Now that it's all been so straightforward and conventional I keep having to remind myself why we're doing this. You just need to check online if you're having doubts, though. Things are going from bad to worse at home. They've gone ahead with the conscription thing. Because we're abroad, we're supposed to register with the nearest embassy."

"Pff, whatever," Tina shrugged and snuggled closer. "For me it's changed. I've let myself forget why we're doing it. The world can do what it wants with itself. I just want to have fun now and sail to New Zealand. We can worry about everything else later."

"That's the kind of selfish attitude that got the world into its fix in the first place!" I teased, giving her a light dig in the ribs.

She grabbed my balls. "Now you're sounding like me!"

"Surrender! *Surrender!*" I tapped out on her shoulder, and we got comfortable against each other and closed our eyes to sleep, light streaming into the cabin through the skylight above us. It occurred to me that, on a boat, we could ask a captain to marry us. That would be Frederica. Maybe I would ask her. I would ask Tina to marry me properly first, though. The two of us had talked of getting married when we came away, Tina liked the idea of a beach wedding. We could do it when we reached the Tuamotus. Would it mean anything? I would leave it to her to decide. I drifted off into sleep.

We slept just a short time to recover our energy. When we opened our eyes, we could hear Neil above us. He had found a can of tung oil and was already sanding and oiling the deck. He had been left in charge of Paz and had put her in an empty cabin, where she was asleep on a bed, while he worked. Tina and I arose and helped Red and Jen, the masters of provisions, to finish unloading everything from Little Billie into our new home, the *Gitana*. It was amazing how similar our needs would be at sea to on the land. Nearly all of the supplies from the van we elected to keep, including the tents and camping gear. Freddie had gone to accompany Nyree and Joe, the equipment team, on an outing to purchase marine-grade waterproof suits, boots and life jackets for all of us, a cage for Paz to sleep in, and new fishing rods and tackle. The freshwater fishing rods and lines from the van were not strong enough for all types of fishing at sea, but we kept them on board all the same. There was storage space to spare. When all of our food and kit had been packed and stowed away, with care taken not to unbalance the boat, and we had cleaned the Kombi, Red and Jen compiled a list of additional food and provisions and left to look for them. The more we could carry, the better.

After Red and Jen were gone, Tina and I took the chance to say our farewell to the now empty Little Billie, who stood in the car park looking as good as the day we had driven her out of Kay's workshop. Tina hugged one of the front corners, her cheek against the windshield. We thought of Kay.

"Would he mind that we're leaving Little Billie?" she asked me.

"She'll be well looked after here," I said. It brought a tear to the eyes of us both to leave her here after she had brought us across an entire continent.

With time now to further investigate the chart display system, depth sounder, weather instruments, radio and other electronic gadgets on board, Tina and I went back to the boat and sat down to do so. We passed the rest of the afternoon experimenting to see what we could do. I was relieved at how easily our charts transferred across onto the chart display system and we were soon familiarising ourselves with its features, aided by frequent referrals to the internet using the satellite set-up. As we solved the small problems we encountered, I was equally relieved that my short engineering career had not been wasted after all.

Frederica prepared us our first meal aboard the *Gitana* that night on the alcohol stove. We were fortunate that the jerry cans from Little Billie, now full of alcohol, would also serve us as cooking fuel.

"Listen to this," Joe demanded our attention, as Freddie cooked. He was lying on one of the bunks looking at the internet on his phone. He précised to us what he was reading.

"In the first ever single-handed round-the-world yacht race there was this English bloke, Blyth, who set off to sail, *single-handed, around the world...* with *no sailing experience whatsoever.* He got some other people to rig the boat up for him on the day he left."

"Are you trying to say that we're not the only people who are crazy enough to do this sort of thing, Joe?" asked Nyree. She was cradling Paz in her arms.

"That's what I was hoping," he replied. "Listen... as he sailed away he had to follow another boat so that they could show him how to sail it. This keeps getting better!"

"What a legend. He should go on the legends list," suggested Neil.

"Good point, bru. He's going on there." Joe tapped the details into his phone. "It was an age ago as well. He wouldn't have even had half the flash kit we've got on here." He sighed, "Ah, good, I feel better now," then chuckled, "I'm ready to set off whenever!"

"What happened to him?" asked Neil.

"*Signore* Blyth? He was one of the favourites of my father!" said Frederica, looking over her shoulder from the stove, where a white sauce was simmering, sending a mouth-watering steam around the cabin. She was boiling another pan of salted water for pasta. "In that race he had to stop near to the Cape of Good Hope. His boat capsized many times. But then, after, he was the first one to sail alone around the world in the other direction, the more difficult way, against the winds."

"*Vish,*" Neil approved.

~~~~~

Rodolfo returned the next day and, without ado, we set off to sail around the white rocks near the rocky islet of *El Frontón* that he had pointed out to us the previous day. A steady *viento alisio* blew across the bay, out towards our objective. Neil guided us the short distance out of the marina using the engine. Once we were in the bay and we had hoisted the sails, Rodolfo barely spoke, allowing us to make the novice errors that were inevitable, and allowing Freddie to pick us up on them. Loaded up with all of our provisions by Red and Jen, who had also filled the freshwater tanks, we hoped that the *Gitana* would handle just as she would when we set off for good.

Everyone contributed their bit. Jen took lookout on the bowsprit. Freddie called orders to Joe and Red on the deck, Joe on the port side, Red on starboard, with Neil on the helm and Nyree controlling the main sail. When the wind blew from our port, Red would handle the foresail, Joe performing this task when the wind came from starboard. Tina and I set bearings and advised Freddie on when to call manoeuvres, Tina monitoring our progress on the instruments in the cabin, and I standing on deck at the cabin entrance. From where I stood, I could talk to Tina, corroborating what she was seeing on the screens with my own eyes, as well as being able to feel shifts in the wind and the water, and to advise our *capitana* on changes of course. I was also an extra pair of hands that she could call on when needed.

We ran with the wind on the way out towards the rocks, and gybed around them with cries of *'Gybe Ho'*, Red narrowly avoiding having his head clipped on one occasion by the boom swinging across the deck, to Neil's great amusement. On the return we tacked erratically into the breeze, performing many more turns than had been necessary on the outward run.

Ours was not a perfect system, nowhere near it, but it was our own and, to everyone's amazement, it actually worked. It was one of the most exhilarating things I had ever done. Everyone made mistakes and everyone picked each other up when they fell, in the customary bantering fashion. The salt air infused us all with vigour and renewed strength after the weeks we had spent living in the Kombi, and we knew that what we were doing was good. Above all, we sensed freedom and adventure, the highest callings.

As we neared the marina once more, we hauled down and furled the sails and Neil returned us to our mooring, running on the engine.

"My friends," said Rodolfo, when we had landed and made the *Gitana* safe, "this has been a fine sail. When we are sailing, you are, what we would call in Spanish, *una banda!*"

I laughed. "That would be something like a 'mob'," I

translated.

"A *mob*! Yes!" repeated Rodolfo. "But, you are a very fine *mob*! Everybody, *everybody*, is a good worker. Now, there is one more trip that we must do, all together, around the *Isla San Lorenzo*. That is the large island that we saw beyond *El Frontón*, at the north of the bay. This trip will be so that I can teach you to use the wind-vane steering system and the safety harness on the mast. We can do this two days from now. I apologise, but I have an appointment tomorrow. After that, you are free to stay here in the marina as long as you please. Just let me know when you wish to leave and I will advise the marina that the *Gitana* is no longer moored here."

We all nodded, thanked Rodolfo and agreed that we would meet him in two mornings' time for the outing around the Isla San Lorenzo.

"I would recommend," added Rodolfo, "that after the *Isla San Lorenzo*, you go to Paracas, which you would have passed driving on your way to Lima, in order to practise sailing against the currents. And then you should do other trips along the coast, before you go into the deep ocean. There are many small bays where one can moor a boat on the coast at night. That is just my advice. Most important of all, please, never lose your respect for the ocean. Never. Friends, we will meet in two days."

We bade farewell to Rodolfo, shook his hand, and handed him the keys to Little Billie before he left with his habitual smile and wave.

Neil watched as Rodolfo disappeared around the corner of the pontoon. "What a geezer," he declared.

XXIX

I brewed ground coffee on the stove for everyone early the next morning, waking them in their bunks. Following breakfast, most of us went into the city. Neil stayed behind to continue sanding and tung-oiling the woodwork on the *Gitana*. Red and Jen also stayed, to reorganise the packing of the equipment and provisions, and to buy as much fuel as they could fit on board to power the engine and the generator. It was expensive but would be worth it for use in emergencies. They had given the rest of us a shopping list of things to bring back. Tina and I accompanied Freddie, Joe and Nyree to the fishing shop where they had bought the rods and tackle the previous day, and we chose snorkelling masks, fins and wetsuits for ourselves. We bought a set of these for everyone, using sizes that we had written down for Neil, Red and Jen, and we acquired two additional sets as spares. We then set about looking at spearfishing equipment that Freddie, with great foresight, had identified as being an excellent additional means for us to catch our own food. Taking our snorkel kit in plastic bags, Tina and I excused ourselves and left the three others deliberating earnestly over spearguns. We arranged to meet them later, back at the boat. In the meantime, we went to look for the bookshop, which Rodolfo had advised us about, where we could buy the paper navigational charts.

We found the bookshop on a busy high street in the high-rise district of Miraflores. It was extensive and modern, with light background music, a coffee shop that sent a pleasant aroma wafting across the bookshelves and a large area dedicated to travel books and maps. Despite the bustle of the street outside, there were relatively few people browsing. Tina and I, seeing the maps section, descended like vultures onto the paper nautical charts and secured a set of all of the Pacific copies that we could find. I felt guilty doing this, as though I was depriving somebody else of the right to use them. For many of them, only a single copy existed in the shop. With the charts tucked under our arms, our main objective for the day already accomplished, we browsed at our leisure around the shelves, eyes flitting along the rows of books, looking for anything else that may be of use to us.

"Oh!" Tina exclaimed. "Look at this."

She put her bag and charts down and picked a large, blue book off the shelves. It was entitled *Rutas de Navegación del Mundo*, or *World Cruising Routes*. She looked at the front and then the back cover and handed it to me. I put my own bag and charts with hers and opened the book, supporting it on my forearm so that we could both look at it. It had been written by a Brit, Jimmy Cornell. Flicking through it together, we quickly found the South Pacific routes and discovered that our voyage to New Zealand would essentially be a variant of what was known in the sailing world as the 'Coconut Milk Run'. It was a course sailed by some three hundred and fifty yachts a year. Many would set off from California, but some would enter the Pacific through the Panama Canal, following a route that tracked south-west from there to coincide with our intended path at a point just south of the Equator.

I looked up from the book at Tina. "It's just like Kay said in Florianopolis, T, do you remember? No matter what you do, there're always a million people that have done it before you. Although it was more like this when he said it: *'Nigh matter wit yerz doo, mayte, there's alwighs a millyun other faackers've got there first,'*" I pronounced in an epically failed attempt at an Australian accent.

"I didn't realise that Kay was Scots-Pakistani?" Tina smirked.

"Ha, OK, I do need to work on my Aussie - that was mangled - but do you remember?"

"I remember him saying that, yes. But so what? It doesn't mean our trip won't be special, Josster, if that's what you're saying. All it means is that there's roughly a good route for us to follow. I find it quite encouraging, don't you? Even if it has been done thousands of times, every single one of those trips has been unique." She took the book from me and scoured the pages, using a finger to guide her eye across the Spanish text. "Look here too. Between November and March, it's not a good time for us because of the cyclone season in the South Pacific. Isn't that what it says? We've basically got about two months, until the end of October, to find somewhere to spend the winter."

"I wasn't saying that it wouldn't be special, T, just that it always amazes me what people have done before. I mean, even the name, the Coconut Milk Run, makes it sound like we're just going down to the shops. You're right about that, we'll have to figure out a way to avoid the cyclone season, for sure. Two months to make it to the Marquesas, barring... attacks by *whales*?" I spoke as I read,

"Which it says here are a possibility. But two months should be enough, then maybe we lay up somewhere for five months overwintering on a beach, if we can. Red'd like that. Or we could cross the Doldrums to get across to the North Pacific where it'll be the fine time of year – the cyclone season is the opposite from the South. We could go to the Line Islands. Or, how about..." I pointed at the map we were looking at in the book, "... the Tuamotus. They look reachable as well. Isn't that where Frederica said that she wanted to go?" We studied the text more closely.

"Did anyone tell her they were called the *Dangerous Islands*?" asked Tina. "Can you read it?"

"Shallow reefs... strong currents... risk of cyclones... impossible to find good shelter... charts that are not aligned with GPS... stunningly beautiful..." I summarised, then kidded, "Our kind of place, there can't be many people there. And most of the ones that are there, are at the bottom of the sea!"

"Don't even entertain the thought, Joss, I'm serious. We're not going there."

"Don't say that to me, T, say it to Freddie. Going to the Tuamotus is her *dream*. And she's the *captain!*" I squeezed Tina, laughing. "We won't do anything stupid, beautiful. To me, it's looking like, as long as the boat's in good shape and we've got supplies, there are a lot of possibilities. Red and Jen have bought enough food to feed an army for a year. In any case, before deciding which way to go, we're going to have to read that pretty carefully." I pointed at the book in Tina's arms. "Getting battered by a cyclone is not on my list of things to do before I die. That book was a good spot babe."

We bought the charts and the book, along with another book we found, containing star charts. The one remaining item on our wish list, a sextant, we found in an antiques store in Barranco, a stroke of luck. I had never used a sextant but knew I could work out how to do so if and when necessary. I intended to learn at the first opportunity. With our bags of purchases and sweating in the heat, we made our way back to the boat, stopping briefly to buy some extra tubs of powdered milk that Red and Jen had requested.

~~~~~

We arrived back at the marina around lunchtime, hot, thirsty and exhausted. We walked through the sliding doors into the entrance building and crossed the silent white atrium, the man on the reception desk not even raising his head to acknowledge us. We passed out of the back door of the building and walked along the pontoon with our bags, looking forward to dumping them in the boat and sitting down with a drink.

Turning the corner onto the branch of the pontoon where the *Gitana* was moored, we caught sight of Neil on the deck with two military policemen dressed in dark blue fatigues and caps with black leather boots and belts. Plastic boxes of our food and kit were strewn across the roof of the cabin, where Jen sat, holding Paz. I could not see Red. We walked up to the stern of the boat and put our bags down on the wooden walkway.

"Glad you're back mate, we need you," Neil said, looking at me. "Can you ask these dickheads what they're doing?" He indicated with a sideways tilt of his head at the policemen.

I stepped aboard the *Gitana*, leaving Tina on the pontoon, and addressed myself to what appeared to be the more senior of the two plods on the deck. He stood half a foot shorter than me and was stocky, with a dark complexion, crew cut, acne-scarred cheeks and a completely humourless face. He carried a pistol and a cosh on the belt around his waist. Behind him, sitting on the starboard corner of the taffrail at the stern of the boat, reclined a swarthy, bored comrade chewing gum and sniffing and with a machine pistol slung around his neck. There was a big gob of phlegm on the deck by his boot that I presumed was his. Neil moved to stand behind me, by the rail on the port side. Jen was still sitting on the roof amongst the things that had been removed from the cabin and strewn around up there. She was looking about her and stroking Paz, seemingly unaffected by the tense atmosphere.

"*¿Qué está pasando?* What's happening here?" I asked. I had no time for petty authority at the present moment.

"Inspection," he said curtly. "Is this your vessel?"

"No," I lied. There was no way for them to establish that it was our boat. Even the proof of ownership and maintenance history documents that Rodolfo had given us did not have any of our names on them. I always felt compelled to lie to plods, even if I didn't need to.

"Why are you living aboard it? Your situation is irregular. We require all foreign nationals to be registered at their place of lodging at all times." He was evidently smug with the authority that our supposedly irregular situation gave him over us.

"We're borrowing it to make a voyage," I replied.

"You're leaving Peru?" he asked, suggesting that he believed this to be the case.

"No. We're going to Paracas," I lied again.

He eyeballed me, his beady eyes scrutinising me from

beneath the peak of his cap. It was plain that he hated me.

"This vessel is equipped for a voyage of many months. You are not going to Paracas. You are leaving Peru," he stated. "To leave Peru you must satisfy the requirements of Customs and Immigration, hand in your immigration paper and obtain an exit stamp in your passport. Give me your documents."

I momentarily recalled how anally retentive the process of obtaining the entry stamp for Peru had been when we had crossed the border at Puno, on Lake Titicaca. As well as the stamp in our passports, we had been given an innocuous looking, delicate piece of paper which, we were advised, if we lost it, would incur us a substantial fine upon exit from the country. This was the immigration paper to which he referred. Of course, a lot of people ended up losing it. Just another racket.

I looked at the plod, not responding to his demand to hand over my documents. He looked dangerous. I was not comfortable with this individual knowing who I was. I thought about spinning a line about my passport being back in a hostel but decided against it. I'd already implicitly confirmed that we were living aboard the boat by not contesting his assertion that our living situation was irregular, damn it. I felt the rage building in inside me and had to control a surge of anger that impelled me to throttle this spite-filled, piss-weak, brain-dead, junk-human.

"I'll get them," I told him. I walked over to the cabin and descended the steps. Red was inside with another plod, a scrawny, rat-like specimen with a thin moustache who was gratuitously rummaging through cupboards and creating a terrible mess. Red motioned with his eyes towards an open navy-coloured holdall on the bunk in which our satellite hub, tablet computer and two cell phones had been placed. I cursed silently, then moved past them, explaining to the plod that I was getting my passport, which in fact was already in the pocket of my jeans. I went into the front cabin that Tina and I shared. It had not been reached by the so-called inspection yet and was how we had left it. I lifted the corner of the mattress and pulled up the lid of the stowage compartment that lay beneath it. Reaching into it and feeling with my hand, I pulled out my bone-handled hunting knife, in its sheath, and quickly tucked it into the front of my belt, under my shirt. I restored the mattress to how it had been previously and took my passport from my pocket, showing it to the rat-like plod in the main cabin as I emerged and closed the door. As I approached the steps to leave the cabin I grabbed the navy holdall. I was incandescent with fury. I climbed back out of the shade of the cabin and onto the hot deck. I squinted in the sun.

"Give me the bag," demanded the senior plod, pointing at the holdall.

"You have no right to do this. It's robbery," I muttered through a clenched jaw, struggling to control my voice, such was my rage.

Hearing my voice, Neil stood up straighter and the swarthy plod with the machine pistol raised his eyebrows. Tina looked on desperately from the pontoon. Jen had stood up to put Paz inside her cage, which was also on the roof of the cabin.

"We have the right to confiscate any contraband or suspicious items for further inspection, as well as the right to impound this vessel." The plod's voice was low and calm, as though he had done this a hundred times before. It was too much. I'd had enough of these kinds of people.

"Just give him the bag, mate. It's probably just money they're after," Neil said from behind me.

Still seething with rage, I did as Neil said, throwing the holdall on the floor at the feet of the main plod.

"Good. Now show me your documents," he said.

The *motherfucker*. Who knew where this was going? They'd end up taking our boat, our kit, our money, the lot. They'd threaten us with being locked up. If they left today they'd be back again tomorrow. We were powerless against them, our only escape was the boat. My heart pounded as though it was going to break my ribs and leap out of my chest. My vision was slightly blurred. I was delirious on adrenaline. I was *sick* of *fucks* like this giving us grief, when all we were trying to do was mind our business and *live our lives*. In an uncontrollable fit of fury that welled up inside me, I decided there and then that I was going to do him. I'd drop the passport, then as I stood up I'd thrust the knife in and up, under his ribs. *Worthless fucking plod*.

I motioned to give him my passport but dropped it deliberately alongside the holdall on the deck, making it appear an accident. As I bent down to pick it up I reached for the hunting knife in the front of my jeans. I had a final moment of self-doubt, thinking of Tina watching from the pontoon. There was a chance this would ruin everything, but...

At that instant I heard a soft thud above me, like a stone thrown hard onto grassy ground, and shrill cries from Jen. The plod in front of me fell sideways. Jen was screaming to Red in Korean and there were banging noises from inside the cabin. I stood up and saw Jen, at her full height on the roof of the cabin, feet planted firmly at the width of her shoulders, drawing back the elastic of a slingshot. With the sun behind her, she appeared a statue. The swarthy plod with the machine pistol was fumbling with it, still seated on the taffrail, looking down in panic as he attempted to release a catch. Jen fired the slingshot and hit him on the crown, stunning him through his blue cap, which fell off. He lolled forward. I looked down at where the main plod was lying in front of me. His temple was bleeding and he was unconscious. Neil reacted more quickly than me, pushing me aside fiercely and pulling the cosh from the belt of the body on the ground, jumping down the steps into the cabin, where there were shouts from Red in Korean back to Jen and sounds of a struggle.

Stepping over the body to the lolling figure of the swarthy plod, I pushed his shaven head down over his knees and pulled out my hunting knife.

"No! Joss!" cried Tina.

I brought my clenched fist down hard, striking him with the end of the bone handle of the knife where the nape of his neck met the base of his skull. The plod spasmed and fell forwards, landing prostrate on the deck.

"He's knocked out," I said to Tina.

I looked into the cabin, where Red held the unconscious scrawny plod, a thick arm around his neck in a choke hold.

"All good here, mate," said Neil.

Panting with adrenaline, we removed all of the weapons and radios from the unconscious bodies of the plods, then cinched their hands and feet together with plastic cable ties, hands behind their backs, and lowered them into the cabin, out of sight. We stuffed socks into their mouths, like we had seen in the movies, and gagged them tightly with several layers of silver duct tape. Finally, we blindfolded all of them, also with duct tape. None of them were dead. We beat all three of them across the base of the skull again with a cosh to make sure they would stay unconscious.

"These goddam' guys were really sucking on my left nut," said Red hoarsely. "Well, it din't pan out as I expected, but that's the way to deal with 'em. It should shut 'em up for a bit, anyhow. Jen, sugar, you are a cracker jack, *super* goddam' shot with that slingshot, no messin'. That sure got us out of a fix, man."

We congratulated Jen on her heroics.

"It was lucky. A slingshot was in a box on the roof near to me, and a box of Neil's bolts," she told us, softly and incredibly modestly. "I could see that there would be a fight, and I thought to stop it."

We linked arms and embraced her in a long group hug, enjoying some moments of relief. Tina had tears streaming down her cheeks. Jen, from her place on the roof of the cabin, had seen everything happening as clearly as if it had been narrated to her. As a wild creature encountered in the woods will look at you and instantly see into your deepest soul, as though you are made of glass, she had seen my anger welling up and acted to save us all from it. She was far too modest to admit it, but she had saved us all and saved me from myself. A thousand times I silently thanked her prescience and swore to myself I would make it up to her. I still couldn't believe how lucky I had been.

"What do we do now?" said Tina. She looked like she was in shock.

"We don't have much choice, T. We've got to pack everything away and leave as soon as the others get back. Freddie's not here to make the captain's decision but I'm pretty sure she'd agree. We can't stay here any longer," I said. Neil nodded.

"But what about these people?" asked Tina.

"I'll lock them up in another boat. I'll do it now. Come and help me Josster," said Neil.

Fortunately, the marina was empty on this weekday afternoon and we were quickly able to break the padlock on the hatch of the cabin of a neighbouring yacht. With Jen sitting on the roof of the *Gitana*, acting as lookout, Neil and I shuffled between the boats, carrying the three unconscious figures across and laying them on the floor of the cabin of the other boat. We kept their weapons and radios, and the mobile phones that we found on the persons of two of them, removing their batteries so that they could not be called or tracked. As well as that, we took the cash from their wallets, and their watches, expensive and durable ones that would be useful at sea. When we were done, we closed the hatch and returned to our boat, where Red and Tina were busy restoring order to the cabin. Everything had its own place, assigned by Red, and it quickly took shape.

As we descended into the cabin, Red turned to face us. "Hey, they didn't find these babies!" he grinned mock-insanely, holding aloft a pair of machetes that he'd bought when we were in the mountains. I was always impressed with his ability to be insincere even in the most serious situations.

"Or my dope!" declared Neil, chest-bumping him and laughing. "It's with the cash in that little place you found."

They whooped and performed a small victory dance. We all helped to pack the last of the things away, then went out to bring our bags of purchases on board. They were still sitting on the pontoon. Just then, Freddie got back with Joe and Nyree. They were carrying the bags of wetsuits and fins purchased earlier, as well as food, and had spearguns over their shoulders.

Joe ran up to the stern of the *Gitana*, where we were standing. "This is a hold-up! Get your pants down!" he joked, dropping his bags and pointing his spear gun at us theatrically.

Red appeared at the door of the cabin, toting the machine pistol that we had appropriated from the plods earlier. "Drop it, punk!" he retorted, waving the weapon around in the air with the same deranged grin he had put on with the machetes earlier. With his wild red hair and beard he did resemble a lunatic.

"Jesus Christ, Red! *What the hell is that?!*" Joe sputtered, nearly dropping his speargun in surprise.

"No time to explain, bru. It's lucky that you lot are here. I'm glad you're safe, *bella*," said Neil, jumping onto the walkway and embracing Frederica strongly. He then immediately got back on the boat and began to prepare to start the engine. "Josster, untie the line, will you?" I started to unwind the line from the mooring cleat on the pontoon that the boat was tied up to.

"What is happening, Neil?" asked Frederica.

"There's no time, *bambina*. Climb on board, we have to go," said Neil.

"But we are not ready!" she protested.

"Joss, can you show them?" asked Neil.

I left the line half-secure around the mooring cleat and climbed over the rails onto the yacht alongside the *Gitana*. I opened the hatch and beckoned for Joe, Nyree and Freddie to have a look. The three plods were still on the floor, looking like they were sleeping.

"*Fuuuuuu-uuck,*" uttered Joe.

"This is why we've got to go, Joe. They're not dead, by the way, just K.O.'ed," I said.

There was no more discussion. I closed the hatch of the boat alongside us again, and the others got the bags and spearguns on board. Neil started the engine and I jumped aboard, bringing the mooring line with me. Freddie assumed charge of the vessel and sent everyone to their stations. Tina sat below deck, monitoring the instruments. I took up my position at the cabin entrance. Jen stood at the bowsprit, keeping lookout. Red, Nyree and Joe manned the decks and sails. We navigated carefully out of the marina and into the harbour, whereupon Tina and I advised Freddie to set us on a bearing of two hundred and seventy degrees exactly – due west. It would take us out beyond the white rocks of yesterday, out of the bay, into the open ocean, and out of the reach of the Peruvian authorities as quickly as possible. Freddie gave the order and Neil swung the boat to face the empty horizon. A strong afternoon south-south-easterly *viento alisio* blew on our faces.

"Full speed ahead," Freddie commanded.

"Aye, *captitana. Hold on, everyone!*" Neil roared, and we all grasped onto whatever was close by. Neil opened the throttle of the engine and we surged forward, the nose of the *Gitana* rising gracefully like a rearing horse and white water streaming out behind us. The wind whipped our hair and the salt water sprayed our faces as we rode over the waves. We were all sailors now, whether we wanted to be or not. It was as Rodolfo had said. The best way to learn to be a sailor is to be a sailor.

~~~~~

We stayed on our westward bearing at full speed for maybe thirty minutes, until we were leaving the bay.

Freddie then ordered that we descend into the cabin, leaving the engine at full throttle and Neil at the helm to hold our course.

I explained to those that had not been there what had come to pass at the marina earlier: the "inspection", the subsequent argument, Jen's incredible sharp-shooting with the slingshot and how the plods had come to be bound up, unconscious, in the other boat.

"Couldn't you have just phoned Rodolfo?" asked Nyree, once I had finished my account. It was a valid question. I had to admit that it hadn't even occurred to us.

"Who's to say he doesn't have problems of his own with the plods?" intercepted Joe. "I doubt he'd have thanked us for phoning him, it wasn't his problem. People like him exist *in spite* of countries like this, not because of them. He'll have had to deal with an incredible amount of BS from the plods to have risen to where he's got to. He's probably a gangster in no small measure himself. They're often nice people. When what's happened gets back to him, he'll understand." Joe stopped and considered something he was thinking for a moment. "I'd like to say you'd have been better off phoning the British Embassy instead, but they wouldn't have given a toss either. In fact, they'd probably have just hauled us in for dodging conscription. I reckon I'd have just paid the bribe. Everywhere's corrupt, this country's no exception. If you get stung you're just unlucky. They're probably paranoid about narco-traffickers around here. We must have attracted attention by being a bunch of gringos living on a boat."

"You'd have felt more strongly than that if you were here, Joe," I remonstrated. "Just because everywhere's corrupt, it doesn't make it alright for the plods to act like that. You can't just roll over and take it. If you bribe them today, who's to say they're not going to come back tomorrow? And the day after that? We were a floating treasure-chest to them. Those were *nasty* people, mate. There wasn't a lot we could have done, other than what we did. It was Jen who saved the day, and all of us, with her sniper skills and presence of mind. Otherwise it could've gotten ugly."

Joe fist-bumped Jen, who smiled shyly. "I'll give it to you, Jen, your method was much more vish than paying a bribe. *Hwighting!*" he laughed, using the entertaining Korean toast that Red had taught us.

Red assumed a serious face. "Actually, I had lost the little bit of paper that we needed to get out of Peru, so you helped me avoid a fine. Thank you, once more, Jen." He pressed his hands together and bowed his head formally. She giggled.

I picked up the plods' radios, phones and batteries, which were lying on the kitchen work surface, and went outside to throw them overboard. I nodded to Neil. "Alright, first mate?" He nodded back. When the coast had disappeared from view he had eased off the throttle to conserve our precious fuel and we were moving more slowly now. I moved up the port side of the boat to the bows, holding the rail to steady myself. I hadn't yet found my sea legs. I looked out into the great Pacific Ocean.

~~~~~

To the people who live south of the Simien Mountains in Ethiopia, a land of bone-breaking lammergeyers, fields of barley on high plateaux, wild ibex, thatched villages with obelisks of giant lobelia and baboons that live on sheer thousand-metre rock faces, the word *simien* means north. To those that live north of the mountains, *simien* signifies south. To both peoples, *simien* means 'the direction of the mountains'. We are heading in such a direction at this moment. What is important is not our compass bearing, but that our direction is that of freedom and safety.

There, in Africa, travelling the dusty highways in the early evenings, just as the light began to fade, I would look out along the perpendicular dirt tracks that joined the road at intervals. They undulated away gently into the distance; slow streams of people in twos and threes and fours walked them, through the haze, talking easily, making their way back from wherever lay beyond. I longed to take every one of these turnings, to step out along every track in the morning, to return at dusk, to see what lay over each of these horizons and to share in the stories of those that returned from them. My trajectory, and that of each one of us, was that of a meteor, shedding millions of tiny sparks of possibility with every passing second, each with the capacity to ignite a flash of experience, but nearly all of which quickly burned up and vanished as they were left behind. The fire that moved forward was the flame of our lives.

There is nothing visible now but ocean in all directions, a dark green, opaque ocean, the colour of malachite. The ocean that took my parents and never returned them. They were never found. They are out here with us, somewhere. I feel as though we have completed our voyage already. I have found my place. It doesn't matter where I am. The place is inside of myself.

We sail towards the setting sun, as I did in my dream. It is a beautiful, blushing pink sunset. They may take the forests, the animals and the fish, but they will never take the sky or the sunset. As the hour grows late, the sun is setting on our world. However hard we may chase it, we cannot stop it, the end is near. It can be sad sometimes, to see things as they really are. I have the notion momentarily of throwing myself into the green water but I hunt the thought down and kill it outright, cursing myself for the fact it has even appeared. To see things as they really are. The wonder that comes with that is what makes everything worth living for – makes it magical. That, and Tina, and the others, and the laughter. I raise my hands up, above my head, and look into the sun. It may be setting on our Earth, but we will never let it set on our lives. Like the once and fearless spider, we raise our battered limbs in defiance and greeting before forces of Earth and nature that are too powerful for us to influence.

It feels like we have reached safety, but we want to make sure and to be out of Peruvian waters absolutely before we relax. I am still holding the radios and phones. I jettison them into the cold ocean.

As night falls, Freddie orders the engine to be cut and the sails to be raised. We adjust our course a touch to the north, to have the wind, which is now a cool south-easterly, behind us, and we turn on the wind-vane self-steering gear. It is easier than we anticipate to set it up, and once it is running we allow ourselves all to descend into the cabin for dinner. As it is our first night at sea, after eating we will take turns to keep watch above deck through the night in case there are any unforeseen problems. Tina has cooked us a one-pot stew of meat and vegetables bought fresh today, using them up as they will not keep for long at sea. We eat it with bread. There is a small bowl for Paz, who has already grown visibly since the day Nyree found her in Bolivia. After the meal, we open beers and belatedly toast the start of our voyage with shouts of "*Hwighting!*" and "*I KNOW FERK ALL!*" and "*I KNOW FERK NUZZING!*" and "*To Gitana!*" Joe holds out Pies, the llama foetus, so that he can join in the toast as well, and Red pretends to give him a small sip of his beer, "Look, he likes it!" which annoys Tina.

I love my friends.

"Wait, I didn't have a chance to do this before we left!" remembers Joe, and he takes a bottle of beer outside and breaks it ceremonially, with strength, over the bows of the *Gitana*. He returns and climbs back in through the hatch.

"Right, I think we need a captain's speech this time. I did the last one, when we set off in Little Billie. Freddie?" he invites her.

She looks as though she has been expecting this and sits up as straight as possible in her seat before starting, placing her fingertips on the edge of the table. From outside there is a *ting, ting, ting* noise of a wire tapping against metalwork in the wind, and the faint rumble of the sails. There is a steady up and down motion in the cabin, and we hold our drinks to stop them sliding around.

"Your *capitana* speaking!" she begins. "Well, I will say that our trip has started in the best way possible!" We all laugh freely at this opening humour, and Red bangs the table with his bottle of beer.

Frederica goes on in her sweet voice, "We have seen the best of people and the worst of people on our way to get here. Kindness and honesty on the one side, and greed and dishonesty on the other side. On our small floating island, the *Gitana*, we will have only the best, and we will make it our adventure to find other places the same."

"When the future is not certain, then we must focus in the present. A certain future can be like a cage. When everything is collapsing around of us, also it is like this cage collapsing, and we have the chance to stop walking up and down inside of it, and to step out of it and to be more free than before."

We clap and cheer loudly. Frederica's cage is like Robinson's *programme*, I think to myself. There is more table banging from Red, who I swear now has tears in his eyes.

She speaks again. "Before we follow with what we must do, I will read a poem, my favourite, which I have translated into English. I hope it will work. It is *Caminante*, a Spanish poem."

We listen, and she reads from a piece of paper that she takes from the pocket of her jeans and unfolds:

"Wanderer, your footprints are the way, nothing else.

Wanderer, there is no way, the way is made by wandering.

Wandering, the way is made, and turning back your gaze,

You'll see the path that no other will ever tread so free.

Wanderer, there are no paths, only bow-waves in the sea."

THE END

ABOUT THE AUTHOR

Luke F. D. Marsden lives in the South West of England. His books and short stories combine metaphysical and visionary fiction with realism and detailed observation. He has travelled extensively in six continents and brings the cumulative experiences of these journeys to his writing. He is a graduate of Oxford University in Molecular Biology and holds a Master's degree in Computer Science. Both subjects have taught him how little we know about the world and our own minds.

"I think that the ability of literature, at its best, to unlock and engage the power of the imagination makes it the most powerful art form. Two and a half thousand years of philosophy, medicine, biology and psychology since Aristotle have yet to produce even a basic explanation of the mechanism of consciousness, or of our imagination. We have barely touched the surface when it comes to understanding the worlds inside our heads ... there is so much still to explore. By writing, I strive to venture into these uncharted territories and to create works that reveal something of what lies there."

Other works by Luke F. D. Marsden include the short stories *The Mirrored Ocean* and *The Isle of the Antella*. For more details, and to follow his blog, visit his author page on Goodreads:

http://www.goodreads.com/lukefdmarsden

44312704R00142

Made in the USA
Charleston, SC
22 July 2015